Dedication

For the old souls, the hopeless romantics, the ones who are awake at 2 am, the wallflowers – this book is for you, you will find your way. Know that a broken heart is only part of your story, of the beautiful novel you are writing. During restless nights pick this book up, on a rainy day or perhaps when the sun is shining and your heart is finally beginning its revival.

Even if you are unsure what situation you are in, we are not all just bodies walking the earth. We are souls. We carry energy. I hope my words can connect to that energy to help recharge your soul no matter what emotions you may be experiencing, or sometimes we just need words to help us escape for no reason at all. Whichever reason it is, thank you for being such a beautiful human.

Sending a field of sunflowers your way.

Demetra Demi Gregorakis

LOVE LETTERS IN THE WALL

Agapé Edition

AUSTIN MACAULEY
PUBLISHERS LTD.

A CIP catalogue record for this title is available from the British
Library.

ISBN 9781786299604 (Paperback)
ISBN 9781786299611 (Hardback)
ISBN 9781786299628 (E-Book)

www.austinmacauley.com

First Published (2017)
Austin Macauley Publishers Ltd.
25 Canada Square
Canary Wharf
London
E14 5LQ

AGAPÉ- (AG-AH'-PAY)
GREEK WORD FOR LOVE:

Unconditional love that is always giving and impossible to take or be a taker. It devotes total commitment to seek your highest best no matter how anyone may respond. This form of love is *totally selfless* and does not change whether the love given is returned or not.

'LOVE': AS DEFINED BY A WEBSTER DICTIONARY:

A *"profoundly tender, passionate affection for another person."* I look at that sentence and disagree, I kind of laugh as well – it's more, much more.

That's why I believe in an Agapé love.

Agapé is unconditional. It is a decision, a matter of will. The key principle is to think of agapé as a verb, not an emotion. Agapé love is the foundation for the best and noblest relationships that humans are capable of.

Love is much more than just feelings and emotions, its actions and behaviors we do.

In that regard, Agapé love is about the values we embrace as a way of life.

Real love, that goes beyond the vanity, beyond the body.

A love that can bring two people together forever two souls, two lives. To find that love is a rare gift. To find that unexplainable spark, those butterflies in the pit of your stomach – to just look at each other and just sense home, it's truly remarkable.

You can love someone and not be with him or her; love failed doesn't mean that love wasn't true.

The journey you are about to embark on is a rollercoaster of emotions, of words, poetry mixed in with *"love letters"* with a modern twist of text messages sent and exchanged between two souls desperately trying to capture love from each other.

These *"love letters"* are letters we keep in our internal monologue or hidden away, letters we write out hoping to find answers. Letters of confusion, letters to loved ones. Its heartbreak, growth, anger – it's the experience that we go through to desperately find that happily ever after. The ride of healing, self-discovery – and resentment, the steps we take to find who we are without needing to be complete from another person – it's about finding someone who compliments you.

If someone loves my writings, hates my writings, shares my writings as long as it makes them feel something I have accomplished just a little.

I do believe everything happens for a reason. God, a higher power, the universe, karma, little oblivions – whatever you believe, don't think that it just happened to happen – there is a reason for it, nothing is a coincidence.

The idea of this Agapé love that I have grown up with in my Greek household, is one I open with you; to dissect, to use, to live. An idea that what if, we leave our ego aside, and love, love big, even if our love isn't returned, we know that one day the love will be put out in the universe will come back to us.

No questions asked,
What if we just love,
and trust the universe?

Finding another person to share your life with is the most amazing, unpredictable, beautiful story you can go through.

I hope you find an Agapé love.

LOVE LETTER: INTRODUCTION

DEAR WORLD, WHAT IS LOVE?

What are hearts and why do they keep breaking?
Why do we search the world for the perfect person?
Why do we short-change ourselves to make others grand?
Or hold onto a heart thinking it's a prize?
How selfish, wait – isn't love, supposed to be selfless?
Yet I think we only care about how our hearts feel when they break.
What does it mean *to love* and be *in love*?
Because I read words and poems
of hearts shattered and souls searching.
Why don't we understand our own worth?
If the person who wrecked you can't see you are a million sunflowers – why do you long for them?
Is it because we believe we can't find another or are we scared of starting over?
I believe we all have soul mates and a person meant for us.
But I do believe that we may not end up with the person we should -
Why can't we focus on other things?
Ending hunger, finding world peace or just being a decent human being.
Smiling to a stranger, doing a kind deed because you want to.

We fight for love, but I've noticed it's mostly for the love that we shouldn't battle for.

So why do we fight?

When I can wake up and see the colors of the world, see Christmas tree lights sparkling – and feel warmth on my skin.

If the person who broke you doesn't want to be with you who cares – you *shouldn't* want to be with them either.

Key word is *"shouldn't"* but I know you will want to for a reason you can't explain – and that's okay too – I have been in your exact shoes.

But you will find as you grow and change, all by yourself **you** will heal the scar you thought was left forever.

Do not harbor your pain and anger and close off the world –

There will be days of crying, and agony – feel all the feelings you need.

Accept the emotions you have and let it be the way you change the world – give the love that wasn't wanted by your person and give it to the universe.

Just think: we live in a world where there are Sunday mornings, naps, pancakes and puppies.

Never allow the person who broke you to have the power of taking away the day to day of life's little beauty we take for granted. Like the way snow falls slowly, or the smell of home.

I guess even in a world of full of hate there is still hope and belief in love, so maybe that's why we fight.

Love.

I see this word; I write this word and I still have no idea how to express the emotions that it holds.

It's a deep black hole that goes on forever - and maybe that is why I will spend the rest of my life trying to find a way to put it in words.

What you have in your hands is not just a story, but a piece of my soul, this is my personal journal I'm opening to the world. You are holding my heart in your hands - please be gentle.

You will fall, you will feel insane, but you will heal.

You will lose some petals, you will wilt, but you will bloom again.

Your revival begins now.

xoxo Demetra

ABANDONED WALLS

"I abandoned my wall, the beautiful protection I built –
let it down for you."

Soul Mates

It was a magical moment when we first met.
Sparks flew inside my head.
Something out of a fairytale book.
We sat at the beach and talked for hours and hours.
It was rather strange how familiar you were to me,

As if I already met you in a dream.

Seasons of Love

Your love was unexpected – like the first snowfall of the
season – it was memorable, but more so,
it was magical – unlike any other day.

I went to bed in my world and we woke up together in
another quite different –
the beauty that was so difficult to hide,
our hearts beating faster, looking out a dewy window at
the earth, blanketed.

"When the snow melts, what will we become?" I asked,

"We will bloom into spring," he smiled.

It is love that can awaken memories of things more
wonderful than anything you ever knew or dreamed.

You and I

We could make love with just our hands,
We spoke without words,
We looked at each other too long to be *just friends*.
Four blue eyes
Our soul was one
Earth and Air combined,
We were imperfectly perfect.
They couldn't write a fairytale more beautiful than
ours.
We were the envy of all around
Because you and I could take the world.

July 24, 2012

*My heart was a sunflower that you brought to bloom on
an ordinary summer afternoon.*

Unlonely

I buried my head in your chest, into the strength of your
beating heart,
and in the matter of seconds.
Fell dreadfully in love.
My loneliness dissolved – disappeared.
It seeped slowly into your chest,

sound asleep.

Love Letter: September 26, 2012 11:12 pm.
Words he sent:

Almost Our First Kiss.

"I don't think you're a Bambi, I don't think you're embarrassing yourself. I don't think you're dumb. I do think you are so sweet and I do think you are so cute. So stop it."

Sparks

I remember the night
we just sat in your car three hours after our shift at work,

just talking.

The conversation started with a debate on which
Chick-fil-a sandwich was better and ended with him
saying,

"I'm really glad we got frozen yogurt that day."

Love Letter: October 12, 2012

Dear Blue Eyes,

I put my hand on your chest, playing with the zipper on
your sweater. Standing in my white dress, blue bow-
We walked towards my mailbox going to say our good
nights.
You leaned in,
I closed my eyes.
Heart racing.
I remember the exact placement of my hand by your heart.
And in that moment, I was light.
You know those moments that rush by you, in a blink of
an eye?
That was this.
Time slows down whenever you're around.
Our first kiss,
a birthday wish alive
and when our lips met my soul lingered in the air –
only for a second, quickly colliding with yours.
Can you feel this magic surrounding us?
My empty heart you filled with stardust and wanderlust

I fell in love with you standing there.

-A Birthday Wish Come True.

23

His Artwork

When I wrote beside you, you told me that you were a poem, and I was the poet – but every time you kissed me, you became the artist – writing sweet words upon my skin.

Autumn Eyes

Will you love me when my *colors fade*?
When my skin wrinkles like an *autumn leaf in the rain*?
When my *body is frail and weak?*
Will you love me *after* our autumn has passed?
Will you love me when the winter blues whistle in?
Will you love me in April, standing in the rain showers?

Will you keep falling,
falling in love with me
as the leaves fall every October?

Promise me you'll always look at me with autumn eyes,
promise me that fallen leaves never died,
that they are *forever dancing in the wind.*

Promise me no matter how old or gray
we will weather each season **together,**
promise me I'm your autumn leaf
I keep falling for *you*
I *hope* you keep falling for **me.**

Please *remember* those luscious hues
the **passionate** reds, the glowing yellows,
look into my *eyes*—
picture me as a sunflower radiating tall,

but remember this mostly
when my *petals* have fallen
when the branches are *bare,*
when there is no trace of fall beauty left,
when it's hard to love me,

Promise me you'll always look at me with autumn eyes.

I don't know how to compose a message without
thinking you are bothered with me,
I don't know how to keep the conversation flowing so
you won't forget me,
I don't know how to plainly tell you *I like you* without
you thinking I'm too forward,
I don't know how to stand out just enough,
but not too much.
I don't know how to be *your* idea pretty,
I always get pasta sauce on my shirt.
I don't know how to tell you
that your soul is what draws me near.
That yes, your eyes and smile are breathtaking but when
the sun is setting and you are alone
I want to be the door you keep open to let some light in.

I see more than just a body of beauty that the world awes
at,
I see a captivating heart.
I feel the longing of home,
I see you,
for more than what you think.

I don't know how to stop feeling like I'm going to
suffocate when I talk to you.
I don't know how to feel when you don't respond,
I don't know how to feel when you do respond..

overthinking is my favorite activity of the day.

And I just don't know why you won't give me a chance.

Pest

I want to pluck all the dead flowers growing in your heart,
and take away the heaviness and guilt you carry.
The anger, the pride you hold so dear of being cold as
stone
I want to plant sunflowers on your lips
so you beam with the lights of my soul
Let me open your heart,
Let me shine from your fingers
All the way to your toes
Carry me inside,
I'll carry you always lighting the way.
No one will be able to cultivate your heart like me
All beautiful things grow to a height,
But when I kissed your lips,

I died with you.

Love Letter: March 4, 2013 10:10 pm
Words he sent:

Honeymoon Phase

"You are so amazing that ya scare me."

"Nothing can compare to the feeling of seeing a sunflower crease open and bloom" he said,
they remind me of your warm gaze meeting mine,
your smile shining lights up the darkest of winters,
I see the way the golden sun glimmers on your cheeks
they remind me how your hands feel pressed against my face - how safe I feel,
they remind me of our lips blooming into a garden of their own,
the way your hair curls of brown ember
No feeling can compare to the bloom of new sunflowers,
except when I'm with you,
I look at you,
and you have no idea the grace you hold,
the way you stand in a crowd and radiate,
people turn to you for meaning, for love – to feel alive.

      you are the world's most beautiful bouquet.
      I'm so glad I picked you he said,

"you are my sunflower".

Pinky Promise?

You looked at me, and I knew you were going to kiss me, but it wasn't a good night kiss - I could feel a promise in our first kiss.

The promise that you would kiss me just like that - forever.

"Pinky promise?" I asked,

"Pinky promise." he smiled, sealed with a kiss.

Every time you put yourself down,
I get so angry.

Do you know what you look like from another person's eyes?
Not the image you tear apart every day in the mirror,
Not the one who constantly feels that haven't done enough,

I see you and I see more than just skin,
I see successes, and accomplishments
I see strength,
I see intelligence and passion
I see someone who loves every creature on this planet
always helping others - but never helping themselves

I see the most enchanting, consuming human that could ever walk this earth

so why do you look in the mirror and see *nothing?*

Love Letter: March 26, 2014 5:54 pm
Words We Sent:

His Personal Sunflower.

Me:
My face is breaking out so bad.
I'm just going to stay in bed and hide

Him:
Nobody cares what you look like
I promise

Me:
You are mean
I care doofus

Him
You shouldn't
You're always beautiful

Free Falling

The world stopped,
the noises went away
it was only us,

we were on the edge
I jumped, free-falling
watching you watch me,

Hitting starbursts, shooting stars, collecting the universe
in my eyes, finally, free from your chains,
you stood at the edge hesitant,

Then I saw you jump,
we kept falling –

And you took me in your arms,
tucked away in a hallway
holding me close,

He said he wanted to write our names in the sky,

***"you are the only person who has ever understood even
the quietest whispers of me. I love you."***

We left the world for a while,
           just free falling.

Let's Stay Home

It was the best, just existing next to one another.
No words, no plans –
just laying, just togetherness, just the beautiful sound of
your soul singing, the warmth of your breath.
Your hands around me,
the perfect capsule – swaddled safely in our own cocoon
two caterpillars waiting to bloom.

I fall in love
like the leaves fall in autumn
slowly and then
all at once,
leaving a beautiful mess behind.

Snow Angels

The world was quiet.
and the street covered white,
the snow falling, so much like stars,
its reason for being was nothing more than prettiness.
Time stood still.
We were lazily standing in the streets and for once weren't
in a rush to experience anything other than being together,
and the sky dusty gray lit up our blue eyes.
*My soul follows you, love encircles us and I love being
yours.*
we were angels glowing, dancing in our own snow globe
around and around.
Snow falling soundlessly in the middle of the night will
always fill my heart with longing sweet memories of that
cold December night.

Today,
I want to go lay in a sunflower field with you
with your hand in mine,
I want to tell you what I think about the universe,
and tell you how I think my soul is made of ancient
moons,
that I believe in a past life I was a baby kangaroo
I want to tell you the weirdest parts of me I keep hidden,
I have had a longing for a human like you –

I want you to do the same,
I want to know every part of you,

let's go lay in a sunflower field,
grab my hand,
let's go be weird together,
I want to lay my head on your shoulder
and forget every care,
every stress,
every worry on earth.
I want to pretend to be super heroes,
and look a sunflower in the face and tell her how beautiful
he is,
and speak in British accents having fancy tea.
Grab my hand,
let's be weird together,

                    sound peachy?

Christmas Magic

I can't say that falling in love happens super-fast.

People say that it's like falling towards the ground – it hits you breathless leaving scrapes and bruises behind.
Falling in love isn't painful.
It's the way fall sweeps in and the leaves begin kissing the ground before autumn surrenders to winter.
Slow and beautiful.
The way we wished and dreamed of snow silently falling on Christmas Eve, the perfect amount to coat the world in magic.

Falling in love is not fast, time stands still when it happens, it transfixes you in a spell.

Christmas magic.
We will always be Christmas Magic.

Forgotten throughout the year but when remembered our hearts grow tender for each other.
The longing of playful pushes in the snow on our walks home, and after, us safely snuggled in front of the fire, *drunk in love.*
Where we counted down the seconds till morning, and for one-day magic is real and the world wears
rose-colored glasses.

Love Letter: April 2, 2014 5:42 pm
Words I Sent

If you think about it when again in our lives are we going to be able to just drink wine at 4 in the afternoon skip class and be lazy? Not for long. Soon you'll be graduated, married and our shenanigans will be faint memories as we go our separate ways in life,
And you'll be sitting at your job and it'll be 4:00 pm and you'll be like 'ah I miss that beautiful girl, good times'.

"Love is a Verb"

I keep hearing that, *"Love is a verb"*.

People say that words mean nothing when it comes to love.
As if I looking into your eyes and telling you means nothing.
You won't believe it unless I do something.
A grand gesture.
That laying my soul on the floor for you isn't enough.
Tearing open my heart and having the ink spill out of me,
as I write you the most beautiful letter,
rewritten hundreds of times, taken months to configure –
that can't be love: love, apparently, isn't words.

Because actions speak louder than words, correct?

Unless I shout it from the rooftops,
unless I buy you every flower that blooms, peonies, in every color that exists, blue, pink. perhaps white.
Unless I buy you a ring with, *"I love you"* engraved around the circle of your finger,
then I know you love me.

Does that mean you love me?
Does that mean love is true?

I can't help but think that has nothing to do with love.
Look me in my eyes, and tell me why you love me.

Use your words, your body, and your touch.
You can move in with someone that could just be a test.
Does that lead to a diamond and a future of happiness and success?
Will they love you when you no longer look like you?
When the wrinkles peek in, and you're too tired to make love, and all you can do is say it?

Love is looking at me and knowing what I was feeling.
Love is laying together, in silence.
Love is carrying me to my door when my ankle was broken.
Love was the way we talked all night till the sun came up.
Love was in our eyes.
You didn't have to buy me the world, or a blue box –
Sunflowers were a beautiful touch, I must say.
But love was when you drove out of your way to see me.
It was when we went to the beach and played in the sand.
The feeling, the connection, the indescribable way we always find a way back.
So, our love wasn't just a verb,
our love wasn't superficial,
our love was the one in movies, written in books,
the one we keep our eyes closed to keep it alive.

Our love was the way we selfishly broke each other because time wasn't on our side

our love was more than a verb.

My Valentine

Send me a Valentine, not a text.
Lined paper with ink written from your coarse hands
with droplets of beer on the edges, smudges from your
mind racing with thoughts.
Send me a silly verse; attempt to make your buried
feelings come alive
decorating my spirit with sunflowers and longing to look
deep into my blues
craving a way to touch each other, to truly reach out and
stimulate my heart.
bring me back to the days of handwritten notes
send it in a white envelope with pink and red glitter,
sparkles falling off,
and I will patiently wait to open it with hope
that I have found a man who is brave enough to let his
heart out of his chest and into the warmth
of my hands.

I want to write it in big letters, and shout it from the rooftops, I want to show you to the world, how proud I am to have you, I want to make you a mixtape, I want write you poems all day and still it would not capture what emotions that live within me,
I know you think it's a childish, I know you think that it's ridiculous, but it is my pleasure to tell you in every form in every way that

Yes, I am so in love with you.

A New World

We all have been at a point in our lives where we didn't
know how to say something.
Why do you want to say it? How do you want to say it?
How a specific moment felt, the days you felt so low or
so high – and you didn't know how to express it, maybe
you burst out laughing, or lay crying.
Writing allows us to freely open our minds to see things
from another perspective, to dissect words that we all
learned from a young age.
Words that are in a dictionary where everything has a
specific definition and meaning – but with poetry
everything is new.
No two meanings are the same:
*The sky is not just blue, the grass is not just green, the
heart is not just broken.*
It all starts with us; that together we thought we are all
speaking using the same words and understanding, a
conversation. But when we come together through
writings, through poetry, we find that we all have certain
emotions, certain kind of feelings, experiences that we
all take in different ways and different strides.
To write means more than putting pretty words on a
page; the act of writing is to share a part of your soul
with the world allowing a flow of never ending new
words and connections that heal.

A new language is created.

Homesick

He looked at me and said,
"Where is home for you?"

And I quietly looked down,

"Well – I live here. I wake up in my pink sheets, I cook in this kitchen and watch the seasons change from that window - I planted those sunflowers in the backyard. I write from that desk I found at an antique store, I escape on that couch curled up with books of adventures and wanderlust, but where is home, you asked?"

Home is when I hear your laugh, home is your hand intertwined with mine, home is your heart beating against my chest. People make a home, not rooms filled with things.
I was merely living,
and now, with you – I'm alive.

So, to answer your question,
home is wherever I'm with you.

"If you really love somebody you don't say a word" he told me,

"I just want to lay with you

I want you to cry on my shoulder if you need too

I want you to smile because you catch me staring when you weren't looking

who said that love always has to be words?"

"if you love someone and don't say a word do you a hear a heart break?" *I asked.*

you loved me in silence, when I wanted you to scream it from your lungs.

Intertwined

I want to stroke my hands against your back,
draw a line connecting us on our bodies,
so that if you leave you have a piece of my soul
that the line will always bring you back to me.

I want to remember the strength of your arms,
and the color your cheeks get when we wake in the
morning, the eyes that spoke poetry I could only hear.

And I'll keep that line on our bodies.

But there is a line that you will cross,
And a new girl will try to draw a line,
It'll be jagged,
Not effortlessly curved like ours
and you'll convince yourself that mediocrity will do.

I hope our lines connect one day again,
because a piece of me is missing
and you have the line we need
to make ourselves whole again.

  Eventually, everything connects.

Love Letter: March 24, 2014 4:52 pm
Words We Sent:

"Silent I love you's"

Me*: And I feel broken all the time*
And I want it to go away
And I'm sick and tired and I missed you and I can't
believe I'm saying that

Him*: I missed you too crazy*

Me*: No you didn't stop*

Him*: Don't tell me what I do and don't think about*

Nature's Envy

Jealousy is a green-eyed monster, they say.
How I resentfully despise the stars;
they dance in the night sky just for you.
How the crescent moon shines above, sprinkling
beautiful dreams to fill your mind as you sleep.
How the sun rises to just kiss your delicate lips every
morning.
How I envy nature's beauty, for it gets to see you every
second of the day.
Sound asleep, in the midst of the early morning when
your cheeks are flushed, hair tousled, eyes groggy,
lashes curled perfectly.
How I envy nature's beauty,
for being close to you – as I'm afar.

I wish you knew what you are, you are everything –
The sun, the moon and the stars.

Sunflower and Salty Kisses

It was sunflowers on a car, to the kisses from the shore.
To the silent way our eyes spoke to one another.
We were both lost, looking for the right direction to go
and every time one of us tried to leave we would hold on
tight.

"Stay here with me, I won't tell a soul."

When you left, pieces of our hearts trailed behind one
another. You took mine, and I grabbed yours; knowing
one day we would need to complete what was left
unfinished, leading us back to the sunflower and saltwater
sea.

We were hopelessly lost, then hopelessly found, and
always, forever, hopelessly in love.

Turtle Speed

Please be patient, I told him.
Don't fall in love with someone new.

I'm Sorry I'm Not Always the Sun,

don't love me when I'm *only* the sun
love me when I *burn* you,
love me when my rays are *too much f*or you to see,
love me when I *can't see* my *own* worth.

I need to you to love me when I'm the **cloud,**
when I'm the **storm,**
when I'm **flooding** my mind with worries and doubts,
I need you to *take hold of me,*
to wrap your arms *around me,*
to bring me back to *this* moment of *you and I,*
to *calm me.*

I need you to love me more than just a *like* on a photo
I need you more than just a *'good morning'* and *'good night'* text
I need to know that you are there at 3 am
when the world is *quiet* and my mind is **awake,**
that you take my secrets and hold them *locked in your soul,*
I need to know *my* words are safe in *your* hands,
that you hold my heart as one of the seven wonders of the world,
the *finest treasure* to ever have been discovered.

I need to know that you aren't *temporary,*
I know you **can't** promise that,
but,
In this world of *instant gratification,*
I *need* to know you believe in **working at us**

I *need* to believe that you aren't a *ghost*
I *need* you to be my lighthouse
when I'm **lost at sea,**

don't leave me shipwrecked.

But if you must leave, leave me wearing a life vest, leave
me on shore, leave me with honesty,
*leave me with my **sanity.***

I need you to understand me, because I don't
understand me,

I need you to accept me.

I need you to love all parts of me
because no, I'm not always the sun,
and sometimes you'll need to radiate for me,

I'm sorry I'm not always the sun,
but I can promise when you are the cloud—
I will **always** shine for you.

I promise I'm worth the storm.

My Person

I remember that night laying beside you,
you looked at me with a long pause.

"What's the matter?" I whispered.

And with that smile, with such proud eyes looking at me,
you pulled me in closer, buried your head next to mine.

"You are my best friend,"

And I knew what that meant.

You were in love.

Ugly Love

my favorite type of love is
where you can be ugly in front of each other.
I do call it the ugly love.
not because you are ugly people.

But you are passed the honeymoon stage,
the rehearsed answers and questions,

the perfect hair, the perfect outfit,
your masks are off
and it's a sweat pants
watch the hockey game
snuggle while it rains kind of love.

Where we can argue about politics,
kiss and playfully make up -
where we can fall asleep on each other
drool left on your shirt.

It's pure, authentic and you aren't being anything but
natural,
and I think that's when you get to be exposed, open -
its embracing our natural state,
beginning the journey to find out
            what really makes love?

May 19th

Please don't say it.
I saw the look.
It was the heat of the moment.
If thunder would crush it would happen now
If the lights went out, we would just feel the heat of our
bodies.
Why did you have to ruin this?
Here is the piece of your mind and I'll take back mine
before we lose our sanity.
Let's save each other the damage,
let's stop it right now.
Doesn't mean my heart doesn't skip when you look at me
when you said, *I love you*, I said it back too –
I added fuel to knowing that breaking each other was
always in our fate –

we are a fire that'll never go out but just tamed from a
distance.

If we get too close, we just end up getting burned.

Dear Blue Eyes,

DO YOU REMEMBER OUR MIDNIGHT ADVENTURE?

You can love anyone you want right now, you can be with her now, as long as I'm the last person you love.

Do you remember getting off the wrong train?
The moon lighting our way, us climbing upon the fire escape,
falling into a sea of blankets and sheets
A playoff hockey win.
Emotions that pour out with one too many sips of beer.
Tidal waves of endless kisses, and your warm touch nibbling on my cheek
you were holding me close, saying not to let go.
The slow, the passionate,
we tried out, my head on your chest
A rose on our cheeks and the feeling in the air
and the words to describe it got caught in your throat,
but all I can remember is when the sun came up
I could feel, with your touch, the love radiating off.

'til we walked out the door, and took our separate ways,
and went on our day like nothing was made.

I will never forget how you made me feel like I was everything that night
and in the morning, how I was nothing.

We loved each other in the cruelest possible way.

With Sad Eyes,
      not as new as when you found me.

Internal Screams.

We just bared our bodies
So why couldn't I bare my soul?

Love Letter: May 13, 2013 8:05 pm
Words I sent:

I trusted you to tell me the truth.

Because I don't know If you do understand, I lose a best friend I lose someone I care so much about and now I need to pretend like I never met you.

Head or Heart?

My head and heart are dancing to different songs.
My head can see what a mess this has been, you have done
nothing has but hurt me time and time again.
Yet my heart hears a different song, one that's beautiful,
sweet and just begun.
Slow motion, slow dancing, our bodies together tight.
My head is screaming:

"Wake up! Don't let your heart put up another fight."

Yet I see you and my body begins to shake.
My head gets angry, floods it with memories of hurt and
pain. It overcomes me, and I swear to stay away.

*"Remember in the middle of a crowd; 'I love you,' he
said, staring at your frown. Your eyes light up, but I'm not
telling you this to smile,"*
my head tells me,
*"Remember how he lied to you before? How could you
think that his, 'I love you' would mean something more?"*

Then I walk by, and his sweet blue eyes meet mine,
my heart hears a song that whispers:
"Give it one more try".

My head screams:

"How many times can you give him a chance?
To break your heart with every second, every glance your
heart just mended, it's freshly healed. He slammed it to
the ground, messed with it, played games, threw it around.
Who goes back on promises and makes you feel like you
are oh so small.
Do you remember the sorrow and suffering you felt?
Does your heart hear that song at all?"

Yet my heart whispers:

"He was your best friend, people make mistakes, don't
forget the happiness and joy that was brought, it wasn't
fake. The instant connection, the sparks, two sides to every
tale. With pain, can come joy; he was just a stupid
immature boy. I'm mended; go ahead give it back to him,
I swear, give yourself a chance to hear that ***beautiful love***
song together, once again."

"What would you listen to your head or heart?"

"when its right, when its real love,
everything is in sync ", he said,

"you'll *never* have to choose between the two".

Eye of the Beholder

I thought to myself, we say:

"Don't judge a book by its cover",

yet we are drawn to the most beautiful flowers and the most vibrant colors.
Imagine if we, the world, could only see souls and not bodies?
Less hearts would be fooled, less broken.
And maybe
you would choose *my* soul, to share yours with.

Love Letter: May 1, 2014, 3:45 pm
Words we sent:

Expectations

Me:
"Okay, let's just make it 'til May 9th and we can forget about each other,"

Him:
"No, I don't want that. You mean,

May 9th,
Then Summer,
Then Fall
   ***in love.* "**

Lovesick

I don't know why I can't find what others have found.

Fine

You don't know what it does to me to look at you.

My heart
Skips.
Jumps.
Aches.

I feel the pieces falling; *breaking.*
My eyes, they burn as if they stared at the sun for hours.
My knees, how weak they become, shaking close to hitting the ground.
My mouth runs dry, words that were once carelessly said, nothing comes out it's a dead end.
Yet you look at me, and look *fine.*
I guess, I would be fine too,
clearly you only break others' hearts,
No one has broken you.

Love Letter: March 25, 2014 2:15 pm
Words We Sent

Screaming for
Each Other's Love.

Me:
Just tell me you hate me and not to talk to you
Go ahead say it

Him:
Because I don't not want to talk to you
Annoy me all you want I'm not saying it

Me:
Why not if I bother you so much
If I'm so annoying to you

Him:
Because I don't not like you.

Love Letter: Abundance.

Dear Sadness,

Sometimes the people we love can't love us in the way we need to be loved, but just because you love and it doesn't work out doesn't mean it was never real, but believe that sometimes our hearts must break so we can go through the journey to find the actual right person to hold your soul.

It's not easy I know. But I think you can only attract the right people when you know who you are.

You might think they are the sun right now; when in reality could be a cloud blocking out your beautiful shine. Surround yourself with your own abundance. Abundance however you may define that, of happiness, of self-love, of your own dreams you want to chase. Maintain passion and then do good with the abundance you are blessed with. Never be ashamed or apologize for wanting to be grand.

True love doesn't have to be a novel with the perfect ending. The most beautiful, striking, forever (in our souls) romances can be short stories – and those are often the ones that are filled with the most passion and truth.

Always,
You Will Love Again.

you keep my heart in the freezer
like saving the last snow of winter,
waiting for the summer to thaw it out,
to bring me back to life yet again,
to watch me melt for you.

Just Kiss Me.

When I look at you I want to kiss you.

Plain and simple.

When our eyes meet, I feel the sparks and electricity.
When I kiss you, it's not just a kiss.
Can you feel the love that radiates off my lips?
The smile that happens when our lips meet?
Do you believe me when I tell you how hurt I've been and
how much you are missed?
When I kiss you, the world stops, I don't feel so alone.
My best friend standing next to me, the one who makes
me feel whole.
But I can't kiss you.
These are just memories I relive in my mind.

So, when I look at you, I pretend to feel nothing,
But I think you catch in my eyes how I still feel inside.

I love you.

And I think you still love me too.
Don't let me doubt you.

Just kiss me,
show me you still do.

One Old Fashioned.

Romance me through my ears and maybe than you'll unlock parts of me you crave.

Ours

Our love wasn't perfect, it had strokes of red,
trickles of blue – areas of grey.
Our hearts were mosaics, of glimmering hues that shined
when we were together, sunlight shimmering through our
souls.
Sunflowers on our lips and when we kissed a garden
would appear on our hearts.

Our Love was Art.

It was never meant to be nice or beautiful,
it was meant to make us feel something.

Silence Is Golden

Please stop talking about love and hearts breaking and the
truth and what I think and you think,
because right here, right now,
we are both human,
I feel your chest breathing,
and I hear your voice -
and I just want to hold you without remembering you left
-
the only thing that matters is that you came back and
brought the piece that has been missing.

Love Letter: March 24, 2014 11:36 pm
Words I sent:

Eventually.

maybe you'll miss me or maybe you'll just forget me
and it'll be how it's supposed too

Picture Perfect

I take pictures of sunsets,
flowers dancing in the wind
soul to soil.
The way the ocean endlessly kisses the shore.
I fall in love with nature, so easily.
Because those simple pleasures overlooked by so many
feed my soul more than the superficial adored by most.
It's a euphoric bliss that my eye captures through my
retinas
travelling to my mind, settling in my heart cavity.
It was when you weren't looking or sound asleep when
you were the most striking, freezing the magnificence I
saw.
It was the careless way you would scratch your head, the
way you scrunched your nose,
And I, today, went looking back through these moments
to see if I could feel what I felt when I first captured them.
And I feel every sentiment, passion, the love that was
growing for you inside –

I look back and our nature is still very much alive.

Love Letter: May 10, 2014, 1:10 pm
Words he sent:

His Plans.

"Well we always find a way to keep each other around, we have a good time, we bicker. Sounds like marriage to me".

Leap Year

I promise
to eat breakfast with you at midnight
to make forts out of pillows and blankets
to lay in bed and just forget the world,
to always keep a childlike innocence to our love,

I promise to love you,
not the love that is always happy and perfect,
but the love that is willing to fight when things get
tough,
I promise to never go to sleep angry,
to be truthful, honest and open

I promise to love you even when I hate you

I promise a forever,
I promise an adventure,

I promise my heart to you.
And
I wouldn't want it with anyone else but you,

Will you marry me?

Love Letter: March 24 11:38pm
Words We Sent:

Reassurance.

Him: *We are never not going to be in each other's lives*

Me: *But why, do you really mean that?*

Him: *I don't know what it's like to not talk to you*
You're my person.

Cup of Joe

It's the simple things you do.
Sunday mornings, in your button-down shirt
It's the way you kiss my cheek when you think that I'm
asleep and how in bed we play
the way we just lay, warmth of our bodies.
The smell of coffee in the kitchen, burnt toast lingering –
both too lazy to move.
It was how we planned our mornings how every Sunday
this would be our world, showing me a garden of bright
sunflowers that never would die.
Swimming in blankets just you and I
until the day we make it three.
How we will grow old, and Sunday will always be our day
to forget the world and allow my lips to write poetry on
your skin
three words are said too much they're not enough.
but everything I need is waking up to your eyes.
And one day,
Sunday will be crowded with little monkeys jumping on
our bed,
you'll grab me close and look at the achievement our love
made,
and every Sunday
I'll wake up with my cup of Joe.

Boiling Point

I wondered if I could make tea out of your love.
what kind of tea would it be?
would it be *hot?* or *iced cold?*
would it be Zen Green or Black?
would it be sweetened, or unsweet?
would you *burn me*, or *keep me warm?*

Our World

It was one of those nights that you are not too sure did happen.
There are no Instagram's, Tweets, or Facebook posts
it was a memory just for us, not the world.
When I close my eyes, I see us play like a grainy montage.
We were invincible, grown-ups playing like little kids –
in our own universe.
With super powers, and magic fairy dust.
We dreamed under the stars, we drew lines in the sand,
everything was possible, we believed in infinity.
You pulled me in dancing close, no music.
Just the sound of the waves, the breeze in the air, the moon illuminating.
I could feel it just with our silence, the faint sound of your heart beating against my chest, the placement of your hands,
I could see it in your eyes the way you looked at me, we didn't have to say a word, we were speaking without using anything but us.

When you are, you don't have to say, you just be.
And we will always
        just be in love.

Wonderland

It's the way we fell into each other, falling into a rabbit hole.
We had tea with the Mad Hatter, got lost on a train,
sang the happy birthday song
Do you remember the way we laid in the sand?
When I was your only person in the world you were running with
There was a fork in the road, and you asked a girl:

"Which way do I go?"

You roamed the whole world trying to find what we had.

There is magic calling us home to each other.

Abandoned Walls

We spend our lives being protected.
As babies our mothers swaddled us till we fell asleep,
snuggled tightly in the warmth of her arms.
As children if we fell and scraped our knee someone
would be there to put a Band-Aid on – taking away the
pain.
We spend our lives being protected, we build walls.
*These beautiful, strong, confident barriers that surround
our beautiful capsules.*

We build them high, protecting our secrets and
vulnerability – hoping some soul one day will try to climb
the wall with great care and gentleness.
Once we admit we love someone, once we acknowledge
love, it scares us that another person could mean so much.
No one wants to feel pain, to become damaged so we keep
our walls up … yet one day we decide to abandon the
walls we spend our lives building and take a chance for
someone to take hold of our heart.

I abandoned my wall, the beautiful protection I built –
let it down for *you.*

And now you left me exposed, naked and I trying to regain
my strength to rebuild – my tattered heart covered in dust,
barely beating.

You demolished my wall.
"*Handle with Care*" the box said, *"Fragile"* marked on the side. But you shook it, threw my heart and lied to it.

Now shattered like a vase all over the floor, and I watch you quietly tiptoe around the pieces.

Too bad a Band-Aid can't fix a broken heart.

Just Friends

We poured wine in a cup,
we sat down and drank up.
Just friends, we said we'd be.
But after cup three:

"Can I kiss you?" staring in his eyes.

Just friends, they will never be.

Love Letter: April 4, 2014 2:36 am.
Words he sent:

Denial

"I just feel weird or crazy because when you grab me I can feel how much you love me."

Faded

It's funny how two people meet.
you connect, sparks fly instantly.
The way we looked at each other, the way our eyes met.
It was like being lost and then found again.
Everything I did, everything that happened I would tell
you.
You were my best friend, my person, my lover.
I loved you.
I could never imagine it would one day fade away.
And It Faded.
We have faded.
Once a masterpiece, full of color and beauty.
Now, just an old picture.
Barely hanging, frame cracked, so unsturdy.
Crumpled up.
Ripped Up.
In Black and White.
A picture that has clearly expired over time.
Can barely make out what memories lay there once
before.
A picture that has been sitting in the sun,
being drained from all the pigment and life that once hung
there and what began.

You drained me.
Drained me of my beauty.

We became strangers, we walk by and our eyes meet.
This time it just feels like being lost.
No colors do I see.

One day a new set of eyes I will find,
A masterpiece that will be truly
beautiful, real and *all mine.*

Nothing

The day you ended the phone call I frantically opened my writings, my poetry, found pictures, looked up old messages, searching for details –
I didn't want to forget us.
To make sure that even though you *(she)* said we were nothing after all this time –
our memories proved differently

   We were everything.

MIND GAMES

"I really hate knowing that I hurt you. I know I did. Again. It's my fault that I'm not man enough to make a good decision if that's what you want to hear. But don't say I don't or haven't loved you, that's stupid – I know you aren't."

Love Letter: May 13, 2013, 10:54 pm
Words he sent.

Letting Me Go.

"I'm sorry I ruined everything. See, just by what you just said, you think about this so much and so far, ahead. I don't deserve a person like that. I can't live up to that. You are way better than anything I can imagine as far as a person caring about someone is concerned."

I'm a broken house
looking for someone who wants to
rebuild me - not tear me down.

Beautiful Disaster

Cry tears of broken hearts,
Let the floodwater suffocate your lungs,
all while he laughs at the natural disaster you've become.
Yet he can't look away because he knows there is
something beautiful that comes after a tragedy.

Darkness

It happened very fast,
I knew it did but pretended it hadn't.
It was simple.
You stopped saying good nights
and I was forcing good mornings,
realizing you left a long time ago.

Love Letter: Wide Awake.

Dear Sleepless Nights,

I lay in bed, wondering, thinking,
thinking,
something is missing.
That innocence of being held by each
other till we fell asleep.
Lightly kissing, cheek to cheek.
My head against your chest,
feeling the beat of your heart.
Everything in slow motion,
nowhere to go, nothing to start.
I miss our noses touching, our legs intertwined,
knowing everything was okay you were all mine.
I miss your strong grip,
running your hair through my fingertips.
How you'd pull me closer with just your big, soft lips.
Looking at your beautiful eyelashes curled up,
your cheeks blushed from our bodies' warmth.
I miss the softness of your hands against mine interlocked.
The truth of all this is,
the one thing I miss the most is
you.

Do you lay in bed missing me too?

With Longing,
       I'll meet you in my dreams.

A night together I think I misread,
and I guess that
if you felt the same you would've kissed me by now.

Drunk Text,
Sober Response.

Him - *I love you.*   1:38 am
  help me

Me: what are you doing? 5:49 am
Someone was drinking.
I just saw these messages.
no you don't.

Him: ***I do***   5:51 am

I'll never forget the day you ran towards me at work
you looked at me and you were making plans.
Your eyes were so bright and your smile full of pride you
grabbed me by my waist, as if you had a revelation, as if
you finally decided that this was it,
I was the missing part of you.

*"I want to bring you to that party next week and I want
you to come to dinner on Friday with my family, I want
you."*

Outside, I longed into his eyes, and gave him my silent
nod, inside I was shattered.
I knew that it wasn't true that you were going to go back
on your words.

**But for a *moment* I had hope, for a *minute* you put me
in your plans**
for a second you saw a future for us.

Love Letter: May 24, 2013 2:30 am
Words he sent:

Selfish.

"Stop, stop, stop

You tell me this like I don't understand.

I know.

and it's all I think about, I know it was horrible

I know I can't make it better, I know.

it's not like that, I tried to explain how I thought about it I screwed up okay, I don't like talking about this especially on text.

I know I liked you so much and I bitched out, I thought about every single thing that could go wrong and I just did something that couldn't bother me. But turns out it bothers me a million times more knowing I did this to you. I'm sorry, I don't know what to say except I'm stupid not you."

Weeds

I was trying to exchange my words for your heart,
but you took my words and hid them away,
Burying every note, I written, every spoken word
Throwing dirt, mud, stepping upon me – trying to erase
everything we were.
You can bury me,
you can hide whom you love,
But like weeds growing unwanted
we will find our way to the sun.

Love Letter: February 10, 2014, 2:15 am.
Words he sent:

Second Chances.

"I know you're one in a million, I'm an idiot, you just are special – I don't know if it's just me but I know you are."

The Boy Who Cried Love

I want to hear you say '*I love you*'
one more time,
so, the last words I can hear you say
was the lie that started it all.

Love Letter: *February 10th 2014, 2:21 am*
Words we sent:

Déjà vu

Me: *Why wasn't I worth it?*
Him: don't say that
you were never not worth it
Me: *Why. clearly I wasn't*
Him: I was just always to conflicted or scared to make that decision.
Him: I know you'd be worth everything and more
Me: *What is it then?*
Him: I'm just always nervous about it. I think I probably always just made the *easiest decision for me*

I thought I was the exception, I believed I was new, different and he would have to pick me, and then I realized I was hoping to be picked like a flower in the garden, like a dessert spread on a table, praying I was good enough, beautiful enough - and I couldn't believe that I was using validation from a person who measured love based on effort, on safety, if you required none, if you could never hurt him - you were the number one choice.

Suffocating In Four Walls.

One night you will awake with this *bizarre realization,* this yearning for something. A burning caught in your throat—it will awake you abruptly in the dead of night—and you'll turn next to you and realize *that your heart needs more.*

You will have a *longing* for something—a *craving* for what your soul told you about years ago but you *never* pursued.

How you shoved your fist in your heart *forcing* it to shut up, beating it to a *bruise*, allowing it just to pump enough to accept the choice you believed was easiest—*to accept what you thought you lost.*

You'll realize how young you were, you will get flashes of the sun blinding your eyes, a whiff of my scent that hasn't hit your nostrils in years, you'll remember my unconditional way I loved you.

You will **collapse** on the floor how you remember you wanted so much more than your small town—that *I* pushed you towards **your dreams**, *to do better, to be better*—but you pushed me down afraid of what could have been had,

So, you stayed behind the line, watching the view from

afar —the beautiful blue sky—the sun hitting the water

and you'll decide it's time to cross over the line with sunflowers in hand,

but I'll say to you, *"it's too late".*

And you'll wake up the next morning in the same bed, in the small town, with the same *failed dreams*, now in a **new** room with *four walls* you **can't** paint, *four walls* cluttered with Pinterest do it yourself projects,

with a soul who suffocates your lungs forcing you to breathe in mediocrity with her as she begins ***getting high off the idea that love is a prison*** —

You so desperately try to hold your breath, gasping for a chance, for a way to change your fate,

"this suffocation isn't made of water, it's hopelessness, it's made of despair, regret, heartbreak"

And you sink under the water, drowning in your thoughts, trying to emerge again with the sunlight of each new day in ***your prison of four walls*** with **no** window panes.

You aren't the same person I fell in love with, *my love watered you differently, we were lotuses springing from the muddy wate*r—slowly emerging, growing out together into beautiful blossoms.

I will try over and over again to recite it like a poem in my mind, even though we can't be together I know the universe tried,

the stars lined up,

the years passed,

*and you crossed the line with those **sunflowers** in hand,*

but it was too late.

In Your Atmosphere

The world is so big, yet all my thoughts are still about you.

Blue Moon

He danced among the stars, and the darkness never
seemed to faze him,
he would turn his perfect face to the world below,
his eyes the clearest of blue jumping from planet to planet
and he settled on the one closest in reach.
But he would always chase the sun.
It was why he would stay out awhile, just after dawn and
just before dusk, so he could see his favorite star secretly
before the rest of the world.
When she turned her focus to him, he finally felt the
warmth flowers must feel when they bloom through the
first frost, under the concentrated rays of her glimmering
waves.
He heard how love was supposed to fill you up –
in a moment, he felt complete.
She let him glimmer at night,
and he let her shine in the day.
Summer was their favorite of time because they could
finally be together even if it was only moments,
where she is slowly setting and he is rising.
For a few breathtaking minutes, they stare at each other
across the sky, admiring each other's beauty.

He always gravitated towards her, but he knew they were
in opposite atmospheres.

He felt he never illuminated enough to stand confidently by her side.

Years after their encounter he returned to his planet and he would reread her letters to him to keep him full:

"My Moon,
I send you a comet, under a blue sky that leaves trails of kaleidoscope colors to fill your dreams. I, a star, dream of being able to kiss you again, fearful we will never collide – my dream is to evaporate the darkness you are scared to leave. For you, my moon, love is light for the soul – and I dream of the golden starlight of blues the night sky gets to love."

In the presence of the sun, the other planet faded away but he continued to revolve around in the same frivolous cycle – he was a moon that never changed phases.

So, the clouds seeped in to protect her glow and the sun was nowhere to be seen. The earth cried for days, flooding the streets while the moon lost his stars and half his shine when he went back to his black hole.

The moon fell in love with the sun, but he kept that side hidden, running, hiding from her – he couldn't promise love if his phases never changed.

He asked the Milky Way to send sunflowers to where she rises in the morning to remind her: they will always be lovers who chase, and miss each other.
But once in a while they will catch up and kiss again.
And when they do,
the entire world will stare in awe at their eclipse.

So, she still shines in the day,
and he still glimmers in the night –
and their hearts are in the same universe even if they are
a galaxy apart.

I Lied

Remember how I told you,
"I just want you to be happy"?
but deep in my heart, I knew I didn't want you to be if it
wasn't with me,
I want to be the reason for your happiness.

Opposites Attract

No two hearts are the same, maybe that is why I struggle
to understand the way your heart beats.
Strong, very steady.
My heart is open for the world, on my sleeve for you to
see, it's slow in pumping blood,
exhausted from the love it's constantly given but never
replenished.
Your heart is confined in your ribs – a cage protecting it
from every flaw and pain,
my heart never was in my chest.
It beats for you; it beats towards the world, illuminating a
fire that can't be stopped.
Your heart whispered sweet lies in my ears and
extinguished any spark I had left,

I can't restart my warmth without
your heart against my chest.

Round and Round

The sun wakes and the sun sets – the moon gleams and the stars come out to play and you still are unaware of the concept of a broken soul –

the miserable feeling that passes through me in a day.

Love is not a toy and do not try to persuade me that you are different unless you can do so with a clear conscience. You never fall in love twice the same way – and I hope one day you will find one that surpasses the love we shared.

Unfinished

"I still want that goodbye kiss."

Dear Waiting Heart,

HERE IS THE LONG-LOST LETTER. IT'S THE APOLOGY I DESERVED AND NEVER RECEIVED.

I wanted to give you something more than just the anxious acts of my doing.

Something other than desperation that will be lurking from these words, settling in your stomach with disgust.

The words *"I'm sorry"* have numbed your ears.

And I'm sorry for that.

But, all I have are words. Not just words, Words carefully chosen for you:

"Actions speak louder than words," you would always say.

I love us for the way our eyes make love to each other's soul.

I want you to remember my lips beneath your fingers and how you told me things you never told another soul. I want you to know that I have kept sacred everything you have entrusted in me and I always will.

You were a dream. Then a reality. Now a memory.

You went on without me and seemed not to be affected by the loss of me from your life.

And I could compare you to a summer's day - and throw Shakespeare around.

And I could tell you how I would grab each individual star
in the sky,
lasso the moon down for you,
give you every beauty this life has to offer;
It won't erase the night in the parking lot,
It won't fade away the pain of your heart,
And the pieces that were shattered and I viciously, quietly,
tip-toed around them like a broken vase afraid to get cut.
But with every fiber of my being,
I have taken the parts of me that were unwanted,
I have watched a willow tree grow,
when I close my eyes, I see yours.
And I want you to know how I pushed you away
when I only meant to bring you closer.
And if I ever felt like home to you,
it was because you were safe with me.
What I feel for you can't be expressed, it either screams
out loud or stays embarrassingly silent but I promise, it
beats every word.
It beats the world.
So please, give me the honor to hold your soul again,
I have no right to request such an act.
I don't believe in me anymore. And you always did.
Please tell me that didn't fade.

I saved you a slice,
and your favorite type of moon – blue.

-    **I deserve more.**

Ghosts

Every lie, every act of dishonesty, in time will come back
to haunt you.
knowing this,
is it worth hiding the truth?

Almighty

How could I have been such a fool?
He was *brilliant.*
A mastermind in the game of life.

He knew exactly what to say to make *me* stay,
he knew exactly what to say to make *her* stay.
He knew what strings to pull to keep me closer, and my
head would scream at me –

*"Why are you allowing yourself to get played like a piece
on a chess board?"*

Yet all I could think of is that he loved me, so I should
stay.
When I think of you, I try to convince myself that deep
down you have a heart in that space of your chest.

When I start retracing my steps, it gets messy-
the more memories and evidence being thrown at me it
gets harder to defend you.
You're guilty of playing two hearts and dragging them
along.
So, mister, is the saying true?
Once a cheater always a cheater?
I guess now you have your cake, but you can't eat it too.

Memory Full

you wanted to erase me as if I never existed,
would that make you happy?
if i just disappeared?
if i just sunk below the water and never returned to the
surface for air?

Dear Society,

HOW CAN I BE HUMAN WHEN THE WORLD IS TAKING EVERYTHING AWAY FROM WHAT IT MEANS TO BE ALIVE?

I sit on the train and no one smiles at me. And when I smile at them they just nod politely or if they do smile, they quickly look and stare back at the glimmering rectangle in their hands.

And we say we want to be humans, and be alive, but our eyes are focused on these little screens, living in another world.

Quickly typing, fiercely reading what is happening outside of us:

Comparing, contrasting, relating, exploiting, judging.

Missing what is happening right next to each other.
The girl with the suitcase, where is she going?
The handsome man sitting across from me – hoping his eyes will meet mine so I can say, *"Hi"*, but he is too busy making love to his tablet.

And how can I meet someone in the hustle of New York City if everyone is looking through me and not at me?

I stare at the ground, nervous, thinking New York is really quite intricate. The fluidity of people moving back and forth, a human jungle, all I see is animals herding through the streets, trampling me un-fazed by the surroundings they cross. The blind eye that is turned while the other eye is on their prey. Everyone has headphones on to block out the noise, the reality, and the homeless man on the corner...

How can I meet someone if no one can be bothered?
How can I tell the man on the subway he has the prettiest eyes?
I feel like I'm watching behind a glass wall, only allowed to observe.

How can I be human when the world is taking everything away from what it means to be alive?

We live in a world where we say,
"Be kind and talk to each other, listen to others stories and learn," – yet no one wants to be the teller anymore.
Because if I do speak, I hurt someone, or I offend, and that's not the intention – I want to engage, I want to help create beautiful things, not destroy the magnificence each individual's depth holds.

But we censor ourselves because it's what's expected. We take words and twist to hurt, there is no assuming positive intent – we always look for the dark cloud.

How can we be humans if we are acting more like computers?
Programmed to wake for a 9-5,
to be simple minded, to be coded for specific reactions,
hardwired to do what is expected and nothing more,

Error 404: now what?

And if you follow what you love you're courageous and a dreamer –
Why is it courageous to follow your passions?
Because society tells us what we need to be *"just fine"*,
and dreams seem to be something that is childish,
so, as children we have been planted seeds of
"nothing is impossible", only to have society rip out our stems and watch our beautiful petals weep over.

That's why I see the man on the train suffocating from his tie.

How can I find love in a world that has become run by wires and lights, where a filter option is more important than the memory captured?

I don't want to swipe left or right, I want to find love organically, like grabbing the same apple at the supermarket and our eyes lock, my soul lingers and finds home in that exact moment or maybe at my job where I sweat blood and tears, unaware of who sees but he notices me in a crowd of thousands.

Why is this so out of reach, yet I can type online what my *"perfect"* person would entail: *height, weight, brown eyes, preferably blue – must love animals*.
Superficially picking, creating whom I would want to date because no much how much you tell me otherwise *this world judges books by their covers*.

The world is still looked at in black and white,
but we are color, so much color.
I'm afraid we have lost the way to see the bright miraculous pigments of the hues which have faded into the concrete where we stomp our feet every morning, ignorantly rushing to get through our day –
merely existing not living.

*How can we be humans if we are alive in a time where **"That's just how the world is"**, is an acceptable statement for the evil?*

Where people kill innocent souls,
how can we preach peace yet everyone is at war with their own thoughts?
And we say that darkness doesn't drive out hate,
only light – we understand what is bad,
what is tragic, what is wrong,
we fight for peace – what an ironic statement.
Yet after all these years, decades, generations no one can seem to get it right.

So, I still smile on the train, and I will tell the boy on the subway he has the prettiest eyes, unafraid to make a fool of myself.
And I will write, and tell my story.

I will continue to be the courageous and the dreamer,
the optimist that people wonder how she stands tall like a
sunflower in a society that wants her to wilt.

And into a world that is numb, stagnant, with pins and
needles in their limbs, I hope I can bring back feeling.
Bringing back feeling, emotions and love in the kindest
way.
Not with terror or violence,
but in hopes that we can get our voices together
and be the generation to make us human again.

Love,
A Human trying.

Double Edged Sword

"Of course I loved you", **he wrote**

"I loved you so much - I had to leave you."

Garden Snake

She doesn't have my name,
but she tries to act like it –
she'll never be me.
you let her head rest on your chest and you close your eyes
–
and when you enter the realm to sleep, I'll be crossing
your mind
like a shooting star, hopeful, to make a wish –
out of reach, shining bright,
you'll be dreaming of places we went, and then you'll
wake up to find that she's not me.

She's not me.

A weed will never be a sunflower,
no matter how much it tries to take over in the garden.

Jack Daniels

when you're drunk
and I'm drunk
we have a connective bond,
two magnets forced together
an electricity that turns us on.

I imagine us in this upside-down world
where you are mine and I'm yours,
an alternate world that sober us couldn't live up too,
we play the same game every night,
the words effortlessly slur out of you,
but we come down from this buzz
it's your kiss but not the same feel

and when I wake up,
you're a wasted dream

Love Letter: April 4, 2014 1:42 am
Words he sent.

"*I'm sorry I kissed your face.*"

You don't know how to love me when you're sober.

Two Sides to Every Story

Fools.
I wonder how you feel with her beside you,
kissing her with your lips of spoken lies,
do you wake up beside her feeling empty
with the same sadness, you arrived with?
When you make love,
do you look at her deep in her eyes?
taking parts of each other souls?
If you knew what love was
you wouldn't decorate her
with tongues of deception
fill her ears with dishonesty to
mask your disguise
a heart that will be wounded in time.
Foolish girls are the happiest.
But eventually your tale will start seeping through,
and you won't be able to cover the cracks.
Life will change
she will see the world differently.
innocence is lost.
Being in love with a boy she thinks she knows.
What a fool she is,

she's in love with a stranger.

Love Letter: Lost

Dear Universe,

I'm trying to understand what my life is.
I'm standing here screaming to the moon,
begging for a path, searching for my purpose.
Trying to find balance between
my dreams and reality.
Trying to find the line of sane from insane
Trying to heal, to move forward
to feel again, to trust again.

I feel as if I'm nothing.

There must be more in this lifetime than just pining for
love?
There must be more than fighting and screaming for
appreciation,
there must be more than feeling broken everyday

There must be more?
Right?
There must be.

I'm here asking the stars to illuminate a path,
But it's still dark,
can't you hear me?
I'm begging you,
please send me some light.

I do not recognize who I've become.
I'm terrified that I've permanently lost myself in
another's soul,

Help me.

Please,
turn on the light.
I'm afraid of the dark.

becoming strangers is exactly what I feared,

you promised, with your words,

"that's never going to happen"

but you woke up one morning and decided
I was going to be nothing to you.

We Confuse History with Chemistry. Falling in Love with a Concept of Time.

I don't understand why we continually hurt ourselves by choosing people who only make us feel small.

We go back to the ones who wrecked our hearts and caused us pain.

We confuse history with chemistry, falling in love with a concept of time.

It's a way of thinking that traps you in mediocrity.

We replay a highlight reel of moments of bliss to justify the pain.

We sell ourselves short.

What happened to our five-year-old confidence?

We believed we were superheroes and princesses, and we dreamed of being grand when we grew up.

Now that we've grown, how much have we settled for?

We go to school to get a degree in something we don't care for because society tells us what good majors will give us jobs that pay a livable wage.

We lose passion because we are influenced to think we can't find the balance between loving life and living it.

We lose our innocence, and we lose that childlike quality of trying to be grand.

What happened to the idea of romance and true love?
What about the grand romances we saw in movies?
Why has love become something we settle for among all the other things?

In relationships,
there's always one who molds the other.

The other person will start even thinking like the other, and a total imbalance occurs.

In this imbalance, you have one who controls the thoughts and actions of both, while the other person just quietly lets his or her partner shine.

That is not love.

We believe **the length of a relationship equals the amount of love we have for someone.**

I don't believe in that equation.

A person who believes in true love chases the *feelings* dreams are made of.

There is no perception of time, there are no broken hearts with the right one and no one is outshining the other.

The chaser of love *values connection*, not the idea that true love equals the amount of time you spend with someone.

True love is more than time spent.

This generation loves the person who can be shown off on Instagram.

Man Crush Mondays and Women Crush Wednesdays are a part of the highlight reel of fictitious images that portray something grand.

But, this superficial love is one I see often.

Why are we so obsessed with the portrayal of a relationship rather than the actual relationship?

I get it; being happy is scary, and being comfortable is easy.

You fall into a pattern of life, and you realize you're only with someone because you feel like so much time was invested.

You won't get hurt, and you don't have to try very hard.

That person is always just there.

The chase is done, or maybe it never even happened.

Love is when your heart has been broken, and someone gives you part of his or her own heart to fix yours.

We confuse history with chemistry.

People don't change, so we romanticize the one we adore.

You are only fooling yourself.

It's a cycle that will only leave you heartbroken.

If history is the only thing that binds you two together, the time spent together will feel like an obligation.

Choose the one who makes a positive impact on your heart and soul.

Choose the one who grows with you and doesn't extinguish your fire.

Choose someone who is your best friend.

Find someone who compliments you and doesn't complete you.

You are whole on your own.

You will not find yourself in another person.

Fill yourself up with your own

dreams, goals, success and love.

True love will find you.

Some love stories aren't amazing novels. Some are short stories.

That doesn't make them any less filled with love, and that doesn't mean the short time spent together wasn't real.

Keep your view of the world through the eyes of a child.

They have an innocence about them that is simple and very real.
It seems as you grow into adulthood we lose that innocent way of thinking that anything is possible.
Once you lose it, you start talking through past tenses of memories.
Keep that spirit alive, and keep that mindset when discovering love.

There is no equation for true love,
but don't fall into mediocrity and comfort with the concept of time.

Eyes Speak Different Words Than Mouths

Regardless of beliefs,
of exchanged words,
of time that passed –
there was a way our eyes looked that said I *still* love you.

Dear Regret,

I wish.
I wish I told you,
not how handsome you were, or that I believed that you
were extraordinary- or that you were simply amazing.
I wish I looked at you and told you from my gut, that I'm
indescribably heart-wrenching, knock the wind out of
you,
in love with you.
But every time you asked me what was wrong I choked
on my words and looked at you, hoping I would hear you
say,
'I choose you.'

Living with guilt,
A wilting sunflower.

Love Letter: April 4, 2014, 2:04 am.
Words I sent:

Capturing Air

"I need to stop holding on to something that's never been mine. That's the problem, I'm holding on to nothing – I'm so sorry."

Miss Sunshine

You lay in your queen bed and she is there lingering,
you go to your blinds and shut out the sun,
hoping you can block out her brightness and forget that
she still lusters in your heart,
and you lay back in bed – your dimly lit room, confident
you are in the dark,
but ignorant that outside the sun is still shining and she
burns for someone other than you.

A Vicious Cycle

Strangers,
Friends,
Best friends,
Lovers,
Strangers.

Dream A Little Dream.

I sleep most of my days, to perchance dream of us meeting again.
Dreams for a moment feel real, in between sleeping and waking – things are possible, anything can be true.
I would sleep forever knowing I would always meet you safe in our own world, our own oblivion –
Until the sun hits me, and I realize,
I'm just going to keep my eyes closed to keep our dream alive.

He Told Me I Was Ugly,

I wasn't beautiful anymore to *him*.
He said that he found a new girl
with a blossomed chest
and dark eyes..
And I said,

"What really is ugly?"
"Am I ugly?"

Was it ugly when I held you when you cried?
Was it ugly when I surprised you on Valentine's Day?
Was it ugly when I wrote you letters to make you feel like
the sun?
Was it ugly when I helped you through your panic
attack?

Was that what made me ugly?
Beauty, yes can be what you see
but it's also in who you are—*your inner being.*

The face you fall in love with changes and ages,
and what remains is the *soul* and the heart,
is that beautiful? is that what you fell in love with?

And if I didn't appeal to his eyes, fine.
But I *wasn't* ugly,

I was his dream, his art and the only way he knew how
to make himself feel complete was to destroy what he
knew he would never experience again…

the feeling,
the vision of his…

one
and
only
soul mate.

I think you either love someone in a certain way or you never loved them at all.

Dear 'New' Beginnings,

New Year's Eve turns to New Year's Day
and I wonder,
people make goals every year before the ringing of the
new day, and I wonder why – because by February they
seem to be collecting dust.

For me every day is New Year's Eve – I believe in plans
and goals regardless of the year changing because New
Year isn't about just superficial wants, it's about digging
within and discovering what you need in this world, in
your life to find fulfilment.

The feeling, the anticipation of the New Year helps us do
that, New Year is truly an affirmation to fully be present
and aware in the year to come.

Those goals everyone has help give us direction.

Without goals, we are just wandering, looking for time to
spend – for days to pass: goals give us purpose.

Find what drives you, find what pulls you.

When you woke up in the morning, what did you
remember from New Year's Eve last night,
was it the drinks at the bar?

The midnight kiss?

The friends?

The text messages drunkenly sent?

"I'm sorry",

"I love you still",

"Come home."

Take a risk this New Year, stop being in your head,
if you want to say "I love you" – say it,
if you want to reach out, *do it.*

Take the risk and I'll meet you half way.

What pulls you?
It doesn't matter if the answer is good.
What is it that moves you to tears?
That makes your heart beat faster?

Write your dreams, manifest your reality,
find a direction and go on the journey – I can't promise
it'll be an easy adventure – but it will be one worth taking.

The New Year stands before us, like a chapter in a book,
waiting to be written – don't give up in the middle of the
story. You have so much to write and its only day one.

Always,
A Work in Progress.

Imagine sending a text everyday
and being left on *"read."*
it was delivered,
it was seen,
but you will never get a response.

---

that's what it felt like loving you...

Love Letter: February 10, 2014 3:05 am.
Words he sent:

Hiding The Evidence.

"I feel horrible that my best friend has a broken heart."

Distorted Views

I look in the mirror and so desperately want to break my nose, and pull my hair and fix my eyes. I stroke the mirror down, feeling the cold glass and fingerprints stringing along. I close my eyes, hoping to open to something - someone not me, and every time I'm painfully reminded I'm nothing.

Broken mirrors are distorted views. Are you sorry you made me cringe every time I see my reflection staring back? Shattered me like a mirror; I tried to put the pieces back. No amount of tape or glue can shave down the jagged ends. You pierce me with every look, thought and breath.

Love Letter: I am A Woman.

Dear Men,

I am a Woman
I am not a thing.
I am not a number on a scale.
I am skin,
I am a heart
with nerves and feelings.
If you hit me, I bruise.
I am not just an object to be pursued and desired
I'm a woman —
Not a piece of land to be ruled, governed, and conquered.
Anything you chase after runs.
Who has been described as appealing, innocent and delicate.
Pure, but promiscuous – **must be a tease.**
Can give life yet is labeled fragile *'handle with care'.*
Some men need a woman weaker than them
he gains false esteem from a woman, who is somewhat strengthless,
as if her inability to move were an indication of his greatness.
To trap, abuse the giving of herself, of her emotions – her soul, till she lies motionless on the floor.
As he stands with a gold medal above her head, smirking towards the world.
I'm a book made with words you cannot understand,

my mind is a dictionary of courage and kindness – but you read weakness.

Her heart is poetry longing for sweet honey, yet only knows salt water.

And he scoffed at the idea of her building buildings taller than he.

Extinguished any fire she tried to start, demolished any word she spoke, any thought she could breathe out.

Trapping her motionless on the floor.

How dare I speak back?

You were the master, and I the puppet; controlled by your strings, caught in a web of lies, your eyes spoke innocence - but your lips said otherwise.

Every woman has different instructions, written in her eyes, in her tears.

Waiting for someone who will read in between the lines.

He was the lightning and I the tree,

his words will be the fire that burned the best parts of me.

but,

I'm a woman, and that can only be defined in any way that I see fit.

But whatever it is, it is whole.

I'm

A Woman.

A Warrior.

Who knew a ~~man~~, boy, she thought was everything and realized nothing.

Respectfully,

More Than a Pretty Face.

Prisoner

You consume me.
I'm a prisoner in my own mind.
Trapped by you.
In solitary confinement
alone with only the thoughts of what if,
love that expired too fast
Torturing myself to thoughts of you without me.
Thoughts running rapid in my mind,
Screaming, crying, certifiably insane.
I'm a prisoner in my mind.
Begging for you to bail me out.

Mind Games

February 10th 2014, 2:33 am

"The problem is I can't tell you what you want to hear. What you should hear. Make you feel how you should feel. I really hate knowing that I hurt you. I know I did. Again. It's my fault that I'm not man enough to make a good decision if that's what you want to hear. But don't say I don't or haven't loved you, which is stupid. I know you aren't."

Reading old messages was self-inflicting pain,
your words, and our conversations were a form of self-torture.
Why do you hate me? Please can you tell me?
You are in my bones, my blood, my heart and I feel like I must tear myself open to let you go.
A part of me does.
A part of me wants you to break like I've broken.
Do you get it yet?
There is a small fraction of me that needs you to feel what I went through.
It's sad that you picked her,
because your dreams *died* with her,

> *you'll be stuck here forever.*

He would always call me beautiful,
but I didn't believe it anymore
why would a bee leave a sunflower
to go with a cactus?

Love letter: Best Buddies

Dear Fading Memories,

I hope you remember our first kiss,
the night we got frozen yogurt –
when you asked me if your yogurt smelt weird and you
pushed my nose into it,
I hope you look back at the night we talked all night till
the sun came up,
the corny love notes I would leave hidden for you,
on your car after work, hidden in your drawers,
your backpacks –
I bet notes you still haven't found yet –
hopefully, you find them and not her.

I hope you look back and don't hate me.

I know you have erased me from your memory but one
day I hope you remember.

At one point, I loved you, and you loved me – at least you
say so, and acted, as if you did, which is a great comfort
even if your love was just a lie –

Love always,
Please Don't Forget Us.

Cat and Mouse

I never would affect your happiness, but it isn't my doing for your uncertainty.
After our hearts stopped beating for each other you walked in the same frivolous circle, and there came times when you looked for any heart that could be one as faithful and devoted as the one you left.

Your mind recalls all the memories and passion of the soul you forfeited and the happiness you betrayed.

Chasing a love, you crave –

I wonder, *will you ever be satisfied?*

Love Letter: March 4, 2014, 2:11 am
Words he sent.

His Personal Puppet

"I like you a lot, and I know I'm not going to be with you. So when I see you sometimes and I think like that it bothers me. I'm not complaining about it. I know it's my own fault and selfish. I like being around you."

Dear You,

You keep asking for my approval
of who you are,
where you should go,
you keep talking to the moon, and hiding from the sun,
you are looking too hard for the answers, my love.

you say you give too much,
you say you love too much,
but if it all comes back to you anyway
is it ever too much?

if you think that your story means nothing,
if you think that without your presence life would be
better,
the cosmos is made up of all our adventures,
your story is a crucial part of this world.
Please know this is only one chapter you are going
through,
I have a novel of beauty coming for you,

Don't stop living waiting for beauty, for happiness,
create it, cultivate it.
Just know that you are on the path you are meant to be
on,

You may not see but you always illuminate stardust even
when you feel dark

I hear you,

I feel your pain,
I have the plan right here,
I know it hurts now
but I need you to know that you got this.

I'm looking out for you,
I have your back.

I promise.

I love you,

-The Universe

The only problem is that there are a few more games for
us to play and if we can make the world more important
for our own reality
than we can be the only thing we have,
the only thing we need,
the only thing that matters,
                    each other.

We would just lay, staring at the ceiling talking and you would tell me what she did that bothered you, that you didn't want a girl like that,
And he looked at me and said,

"why can't all girls be like you?"

And in that moment, my heart fell out of my body into his hand and I never got it back since.

Is she your best friend?
    "No", he whispered, *"you are"*
Can we just slow down time? I asked.

    *"Yes, just **You and I**."*

Reunited

His eyes said, *"I'm sorry"*,
Yet all I could hear was my heart saying,

"Whatever you do, don't go back to what broke you."

Unrequited

My question is, did we not spend days and nights before
the day we left each other – which gives every reason to
believe that we actually loved each other?
That we promised we were going to meet again?
Were your words not kind and hopeful?
Did you not tell me all your mistakes and faults – and
promised me that they would never happen again?

I do not need these questions to be answered for me, but
for your own conscious.

Love Letter: April 25, 2014, 5:37 pm
Words he sent:

Tease

Him: *What do you want from my life?*
  my love?

Me: *You can't give me what I want.*

Matiasma (Evil Eye)

The evil eye is the worst,
dizziness, headaches,
you tear me down under your breath
consciously crafted to preach peace yet you're at war with
your own thoughts, wearing a mask to hide the sun.
Evil Eyes live life with blinders on, sunglasses always
hiding away from the light.
Using their glare of jealous admiration
in hopes to get the prize,
if he is the prize,

you already lost.

Love Letter: Seeking Answers.

Dear Pain and Pleasure,

All we have are flashes of moments, lightning of emotions that strike us out of nowhere.

When I trick my mind that I'm okay is when I get a shock, a flash of you.

That haunts me through my day sending shivers up my spine.

I get this heaviness in my eyes, and they begin to water and my chest feels full and my throat gets tight –

I don't know how to write it, I'm sorry. I can't make it sound pretty, or lyrical.

You never understood my poetry, the way my heart loved, the way I looked at life, but I miss you, please let me know what happened.

If there was a way for you to read this, and get the wind knocked out of you so you could understand, I would write it – but this is me exposed and open.

Plainly and easily telling you – you were my best friend, you broke me and I wish I knew what I did to deserve it.

Did that send shivers up your spine?

Answer me,
Restless Mind.

Tunnel Vision

He fell for what he called *"the attractive distractor,"*
the choice that is almost but not quite right.

Vaulted Memories

Have you ever been in a place and now that place is not just another place?

It holds a memory.

No matter how much you don't want it to mean something, it does.

The room is spinning – my mind races and moments are flashing through.

It's opening a closed vault.

I think of the time I drew the line in sand and told him not to cross it – but he put his foot past anyway.

Every time I sit in the café hoping to see his face.

Searching the crowd, hoping he walks in the door.

That table to the far left will always be the place I surprised him on Valentine's Day.

The booth in the front will always be where we sat and read till 1 am.

The parking lot outside will always be the place he swooped me off my feet into the strength of your arms – almost our first kiss.

The path outside will always be where we playfully pushed each other in the winter snow, just wanting to touch each other and be held close.

I wish these places were just that – places.

Just a table in a cafe, a booth or a place to park cars.

The truth is there was a click, a spark – and my mind
recalls it when I enter the vault – but I don't want to see
you everywhere I go.
Even when the present tells me things have changed
I will always remember the last place I saw him
the last kiss that lingers on my lips and how

he never had the strength to tell me he was leaving will be
the place I remember him the most.

Translation

This isn't logical, its love.
So it may not make sense.
But, I tell you to leave me be.
Go away; never talk to me again, set me free.
But now I have three words for you:

I hate you.

Translation: *I love you.*

Come back, why didn't you fight for me?

Liar

*"No matter what happens to us, if you need anything I'll
be there".*
Why do *(did)* people *(he)* lie?
Because the truth hurts.
The truth is,
All we have is ourselves.

How can you tell me you are in love with me and be with another?

Why give the best to the one who makes you feel nothing but pleasure?

Emotional connection you lack,

pleasure is seeking,
         sought and
                  had.

I know you think of me.

Web

It was the way you spoke to me,
softly.
The way you smiled.
Even the way you ignored me.
That was just so exhilarating.
That caught me in your web,
a tiny fly who was
entangled by your lust
dying for a bite.

Another Life

'Do you ever wish we were older when we met?' I asked.

"No. I'm glad we met, what do you mean?"

'I wish I met you five years from now, so maybe we could still have a chance because I look at you, and I wish we could start over.'

"Start over?" he asked.

'So I could be the girl you wanted forever, and you are the man you need to be before meeting a girl like me.'

Monster

I used to take the parts of you I wanted to remember,
the memories,
the train rides, the sunflowers, the words you spoke.
Sewed them all together and
made a man that didn't exist.
A monster I created in my mind.
I fell in love with memories, sensations, and the idea of
you.
The creation I made of you.
I didn't fall in love with you.

The inflammation had reached my heart.
my soul is now a puddle on the ground,
there is an emptiness I feel,
i throw up hearts
i cry,
i scream.

Irony

I never heard someone contradict words as much as you,
how they viewed their life –

Who they would marry, the *"standards"* you snicker
about, believing you are above, crafting the perfect human
as if women were pieces to be put together to create your
very own Barbie doll.

But you chose below,
so why, my dear friend do you spit fire
when you have no spark?

Disguise

I sit here and play pretend,
like a little girl playing dress-up, a princess with a crown,
ruling her kingdom: or as a superhero, saving the city
from disaster, zipping around the house, smiling,
giggling, living happily ever after, no one stepping on my
cape.
'til the night comes and that's when it hits me when I take
off my crown, and tuck away my cape, a black shadow
that starts sweeping in.
When I close my eyes to sleep, is when you come back in
my mind and I think of how happy you are without me,
and I still destroyed inside.
But no one knows because they see a girl with a crown,
and a cape.
I wear my smile towards others,
saving their days,
but inside I break.

All Night (...) Till The Sun

Your eyes staring at your phone groggy - even though your eyelids are drooping you don't have to force yourself to stay awake.

You're looking at those three little dots across the screen, *it's a buzz, an adrenaline rush.*

(...)

The talking all night, the indecisiveness of which emoji to send,
the silent smile in the dark of your room lit up from those three dots.

(...)

there is something so secretive about being awake together when the rest of the world is sleeping,
a bond that is created,
something so freeing about two people sharing inner thoughts, sacrificing sleep to talk about everything and nothing.
Even though you're alone you don't notice,
you don't feel it,
because of those three dots,

(...)

Till the sun comes up,
and then they disappear
and now you're wondering who those dots are lying
awake with now.

(???)

I'm still feeling used,
and time has gone by but I'm frozen watching silently the
world around me,
it's like being swallowed by the universe
in a black hole, I live my days
I heard about the sun but haven't seen her in years.

I'm convinced I met the love of my life at the wrong time,
what a tragedy that is.

People's Perceptions

We can't control the way people perceive us; it's a reflection of their state of mind, their insecurities and their own challenges they are battling. My intentions are good and my words are authentic, I can't make everyone love me – but I will be me, and I will always be a kind, true heart – most importantly radiating tall as a beautiful sunflower.

"I don't understand why every flower I pick dies", he said
to me.

*"You love the flower for its beauty, and once she begins
to   wilt - you   go   and   pick   another,"* I   said,

as
my
last
petal
fell
into
his
hand.

Love Letter: October 11 2014, 1:52 am
Last Words I sent:

Flat Lined

"Are you satisfied? Are you happy? Have you hurt me enough? How could you be so cruel to me? I don't know why you came to ruin my birthday... You hurt me, broke me, I did nothing to you. Nothing to you.

What do you want from me? Haven't you tortured me enough?

I've done nothing but give you everything, we were best friends at one time."

The Ghost of You

You never bothered to tell me why you left,
it was those kinds of endings of take everything and
disappear –
but I don't care anymore why,

I'm just happy that you did.

UNCHAINED HEART.

---

*"Our story binds us, we both moved on, but even when
we try to forget each other
Our love will remember."*

Love Letter: My Revival

Dear Lost Hope,

Having My Heart Broken Was The Best Thing That Happened To Me.

You can only correct or heal what you are ready to acknowledge, accept and release.

I want you to know that whoever broke you, whatever cruel person who couldn't gently put your heart back together, is just a coward.

Having my heart broken was the best thing that happened to me. I lost myself.

I want to make beautiful things, even if nobody cares. You must have this indescribable passion in your gut. It's crying and punching, trying to be heard and seen but constantly being told, *"You're not good enough,"* and *"It'll never happen."* I want to add meaning. I look in New York crowds, and it scares me. I hate seeing the monotony of people walking back and forth and the facial expressions of people looking so dismayed.

In the grand scheme of things, I thought I didn't add a lot to this world, that I was just another face to be seen: a girl with curly hair and big blue eyes.
I draw a line, connecting all the people I've met to me.

The line is very long; it intertwines and adds name after name. Would someone really miss me if I weren't here? Would lives be affected? Stories changed? Would my mom be able to wake up morning, after morning? Would the kid I sat next to in my lecture notice? Would my dad drink his pain away? Would the boy I loved regret telling me I'm nothing when I'm no longer here?

I have this thirst. I want to change my story, and I want people to feel at home when they look at me. I used to think I wanted to find a boy who would whisk me away to a castle on a white horse, and we'd live happily ever after. But when I did find that boy, he tore up my heart, threw it in the air like confetti and puffed out his chest because he thought he was a man for pressing, *"end"* on a phone call. I knew that would be a part of my history, but not my whole story.

No longer did I want to be the girl who found love, but who gave it. I want people to know my name and associate it with herself and her accomplishments, who had someone say *"because of you I didn't give up"*.

My history will be a human who brings back faith and hope to a world who celebrates anger, lies, and sadness. This isn't a piece of bashing love; this is me about being a life. I'm healthy; ability to make movements, move mountains and I'm going to stand here and write to you about heartbreak? Yeah, it broke, but I fixed it.

It just means that bigger things are meant for me.

*I can't thank him enough for leaving me behind because I was ready to give him **everything**.*

It just means bigger things are meant for me. My scar is nothing to be seen, and I'm going to mark this world with the love he didn't want.

I'm going to give it to the moon, the stars, and the universe.

He will never fully realize what it was like to feel my broken spirit. I won't say broken heart anymore because it's too cliché, and it was more than that which had broken. But even though he will never know what it was like to put myself back together every day, he will also never know the woman I have become.

There are moments that stick with you and shape who you become. I have this life, and I have the opportunity to make history.

Write your own story.

Everything comes full circle. I am who I am because of the experiences I go through. So, yes, my spirit was broken for a little, but I'm not going to waste another breath giving that boy more credit than he deserves.

We will change this world. Some may sit, laugh and grin, but I know my broken spirit is only part of my history. My story will be one for the books.

For anyone doubting him or herself, the pain we endure will be worth creating the story you are meant to write.

Be grand, be fearless, and be your own author of your very own book.

You will find the most indescribable love, and that coward, who broke you, will be nothing but a transition paragraph to the novel you are going to be writing.

Love always,
A Recovering Heart.

Healing

The soul and body knows how to heal itself,
with a trauma, an injury
mother nature kicks in,
it was never my body that couldn't heal,
but my mind,
the problem is erasing the thoughts,
silencing the ever flow of memories.

On The Edge.

I went from talking to you, to seeing you every day.
To nothing,
cold turkey.
No words, no explanation.
you left me alone in my thoughts of *"what ifs"* and
doubting everything I knew, everything I' am.

Do you know how that screws up a person?
Do you know the withdrawal that has to happen?

You can say *"I'm Sorry"* a million times but your words
are nothing
your actions proved everything.

I'm clean, I'm sober from your love -
please I'm begging walk away,
because one touch from you,
      I'll relapse.

Two Journeys,
One Heart

The last message he left broke my heart, and left me hope:

"Let yourself move to the next chapter in life when the time comes, don't remain stuck on the same page – I'll meet you at our happily ever after."

Reborn

I have been sheltered all winter long.
Withdrawn from a face I knew,
a love that I thought was true
meant nothing to a boy I knew.

A smile that has not seen the light of day
only knows the darkness of winter that cuts short to our
days. My eyes, which have lost their glow
a memory that relapses of pain and sorrow
of a broken heart, and body frozen cold
the reminded of the winter wind smacking me to a fold.

Yet I awoke this morning to the sound of birds,
singing a song I have missed and didn't know could still
be heard. The sun trickling in my window,
I see the grass dance in the wind.

And behold,

a beautiful flower budding from the ground.
I stare in disbelief, how could something so delicate
survive without love or heat?
Her petals of blue beauty glimmers in the sun
leaving the cold winter behind, it's done.
Waiting for a hand to handle with care.

A beautiful flower, not like the others so very rare.

Reborn from the sorrow of winter,
rejoices in the spring day
knowing that love will find her.
Somewhere, someday.

October Night
Nostalgia

I close my eyes and try so hard to remember that innocence between us, our firsts.
And when I think of my birthday night – it comes back like a vivid dream.

The anger and heartbreak sleep – because, for a short time, I was yours, you were mine.
It was without a doubt a beautiful friendship, overwhelming love.

How can love just die?

How Did You Know
You Loved Him?

His eyes.

"His eyes weren't blue." I said.
"How did you know you loved him?" they asked me
"His eyes weren't blue." I said.

She compares his eyes to the ocean,
and I never understood why,
his eyes weren't *blue* when I loved him.
They were *miniature galaxies,*
I saw *his soul, his hurt, his happiness, his fear*s—
Everything he tried to hide would come out through his
eyes,
light beams that would **hit me**—and with one gaze at
each other
there was no doubt, with one look, our love hit each
other like a shooting star,
stardust was *illuminating* our veins, our hearts beating in
sync.
If we ever got lost,
we would just look into each other's stars—
always finding our way back home.

she says his eyes are blue like the sea?
Endless possibilities?

**"His eyes are blue because he looks at her and misses
me." I said.**

My mother's eyes looked defeated *I'm so disappointed in you* she said.
How could you let someone do this to you? Have you lost your mind?
A pain she desperately warned me about, a hurt she knew she couldn't take away.
I foolishly turned my eye, ignoring everything she pointed out, every sign she questioned.
I began to cry when I collapsed into her arms
I thought he loved me I breathed,
I don't recognize who I have become.

I'm not this girl.

He does love me.
He does,
He did.

Trying to convince myself that this suffering this effort was worth it

He took parts of me,
He was the one who knew me,
I have never talked a day without him,
What if I never find that again?
What if I never love again?
Why didn't he want me?
He said he wanted me.

No one can take anything from you she said,
You are not defined by a person who cannot see clearly
the most incredible woman that is before me,
You are not defined by any person who doesn't know your
worth,
he will forever live with half-filled love.
He will never experience love again the way you give
unconditionally.

But one day,
you will meet a new person who will change
everything you've ever written,
everything you've ever felt,
you'll find out that you thought you knew what love was
and you will see
you had no idea what *love* was.

Keep blooming my sunflower.

he lost,
he lost you.

      You lose nothing.

I pray to God,
I pray for answers,
I pray for a path to lead me back to you.
I pray for a path away,

I pray for my sanity back.

Memory Jar

There are these little moments that I wish I could put into jars and open them up so I could re-live you.

I'm not one for reminiscing,
but there's something about us –
I'm trying to remember and I can't.

I wish I could take everything we were, the little pieces.
The innocent nights,
the way our lips fell together effortlessly
and put them in a jar.

So when I feel you fleeting, and I feel you forgetting us I can open the jar and in the air your soul gets hit with memories of me –
an explosion you can't escape.

And I can re-live what my heart wanders to the most

you.

Starry Night.

**The woman you have after me will be a plagiarized
poem of who my soul is.**

She will suddenly begin to try to write poetry,
She will attempt to make the *'love'* you have sound like a
sweet song,
she will try to delete the words that I've left inscribed on
your body, burning every love letter I've written to you,
she will try to kill all the sunflower seeds I left planted on
your lips,
erasing any memory of me in you.

But you know that her words will never strike you in the
chest like mine did,
leaving you gasping,
leaving you craving me.
Her peonies will never be as elegant, as innocent, as pure
as the sunflower that illuminates my soul.

She will never grab you the way I did,
She will never kiss you with such passion, with such a
want,
She will never with one touch make you feel insane,
make you feel how much another person could love
another human, make you feel like you want.

She will forever be a sorry substitute of the woman you
walked out on,

   there is only one original Starry Night –
she will always be a copy of a masterpiece in your eyes

You leaving me with nothing,
gave me everything.

My hope is to preserve from our love, not fall from it

People tell me there is beauty in being alone.

There is nothing romantic about laying on your
bathroom floor screaming out for a name
who no longer acknowledges your existence,
there is nothing pretty about the tears you wipe from
your eyes as you pray for a way out of your mind,
nothing satisfying about feeling like the world is on your
shoulders and no one is there to help you breathe.

inhale

.

.

.

exhale

.

.

.

inhale

.

.

.

exhale

.

.

.

.

place your hand on your heart.

You are alive.
feel each beat, feel each breath.

Close your eyes.

You have wanderlust in you,
you walk on stars, and smile light beams,
you are magic.

you are not alone,
I will help you breathe.

there
       is
          beauty
               in
                    you.

Where Does Love Go When We Break Up?

People are confusing heartbreak with anger, sadness, or 'obsession' of past love gone. Let me correct you, this world is obsessed with love: you, me, him, her. People who are not heartbroken are obsessed with love - with keeping it. The heartbroken aren't a disease that can't be cured - the heartbroken are the strongest most beautiful misunderstood group. They have loved and lost, been alone and grown.

They search for many answers, especially:
"Where does our love go when we break up?"
Humans crave closure.
Love doesn't go away; it doesn't have feet it can't run. Those feelings created, molded for that one person don't disappear overnight, they seem to be left lingering in the air - nowhere to go, the love is left in a directionless way hoping to find its way back to them, but more so it doesn't make it and you are left heartbroken - feeling lost, wandering to get back home.

You invested time, emotion & energy into this soul. But remember there is a bond between you and this person that is unique, that is unlike anyone else - and that love will always be there, not just in you, but in them as well.

What if they have moved on you might ask? You feel hurt, you feel like this person must be better than you, you start to tear yourself apart piece by piece.

Let me stop your self-abuse right now. No one can compete with the love you two had.

That new person who you think replaced you - didn't. You can't be replaced; there will always be only one you. They might try to replicate what you two had, but there is only one original Starry Night and you'll always be the masterpiece foolishly left behind.

Don't think that when they hear that song you sung in the car together or smells that perfume you used to wear, or finds those letters you gave that their heart doesn't flutter, that their mind doesn't race back to your smile, to all the jokes and adventures you went on - or even simpler when they look at nature and see a sunflower that they don't think of how you radiated in their eyes - they do.

You are missed, just as you are missing them.

Believe and know that you are enough,
love lost is not love failed.

I look at you and I don't see someone heartbroken, or obsessed I see someone who loves selflessly and that's the most breathtaking love from the purest soul.

You put someone first before yourself. But now it's your turn to tuck that love into the back of your heart and move forward. I know you're in pain, I know you love them and guess what? They loved you too.

Sometimes we selfishly break each other because time wasn't on our side, or maybe there is another complicated reason for the way your heart broke. Whatever happened, remember you are loved, you are stunning, inside and out - keep that heart on your sleeve. Go live, really live there is so much to see in this world than just those eyes you crave.

You'll find a new love that surpasses the one who broke you.

Finding a soulmate is beautiful but finding yourself is life changing.

Perhaps loving someone has nothing to do with being with them forever, but caring about them forever.
A Selfless love.

And remember if someone asks:
"Where does love go when you break up?"

I say the relationship, the friendship might end, but true love never dies, never leaves.
It stays living underneath it all.

In Love With Love.

Sometimes I think that everything I do is propelled by my fear of being alone.

I need someone to grab me and say:

*"I'm going to be there for you,
I'm not going to leave when it gets hard." she cried*

Please, open the door.

When I say, I *love you* it's because I mean it.
when I'm mad at you - I'm going to tell you I'm mad at you
I'm not going to play these games.
I'm not going to take pieces of you and trail them around the world hoping that you find each piece again
making you lose your mind searching for me.
I'm going to be right here.
I am not going to be an X on the treasure map you need to find

We are the treasure, we will take on each year, each adventure together,
hand in hand.

I'm not going to leave you huddled up on the floor crying,
but you need to be able to let me in.

I keep knocking
I hear your faint breaths on the other side,
your mumbled words of *"I was hurt, I lost myself"*.

Please open the door.

If you keep that door closed
you will be alone.
That won't be from a heart unable to feel again,
that will be from you.
unable to see,
a new soul, exposed,
asking for a chance,
to hold you, to love you,
to prove that your past hurt is an over-sung song.

I promise if I ever should leave, I will take you with me.

I'm here for you,
I'm not leaving.

Please.
Open the door.

Dear Failure,

I think that our society is majorly broken. And one of the problems is the fear of failure that is instilled in our minds from the very beginning of our lives. Failure is one of life's greatest gifts. I have failed, and it taught me what I wanted and what I didn't – from failing a course, failing friendships, to relationships. Failure is the best teacher if we are willing to listen, learn, and go forward. Never, ever, ever be afraid of failing. Because when you leave college there is no *"withdrawal"* or *"drop this course"* button. In life; true success, true greatness, true love only ever comes from learning from our mistakes.

Love,

Success.

that was it, she thought that love consumed you,
that you waited for a white horse and
a frog to turn into a prince,
that you burned for another soul,
till her light went out
and she realized no one is going to save her,
but herself.

Dear Birthday Boy, (A Year Older You)

Today is your birthday and I don't know what to do.
Are you supposed to call the people you love, when you know they don't love you?

Even at midnight I wanted to call, to be honored to be the first one to wish you a Happy Birthday.
I wrote a message ready to hit send.
365 days have passed and I wonder: the memories you made, are you fighting for your dreams?
Or did you settle and put them away?

I found a picture of us on our very first birthday adventure, the innocence between us started to come back. Nostalgia filled my chest and it reminded me how you planted sunflowers in my lungs – although they are beautiful, I still can't breathe.

My birthday wish for you:

I wish you happiness since you left.
Not the fleeting kind we get, glimpsed from day to day from superficial things but the one we talked about, the happiness we dreamed of.
The one that wakes you up in your beautiful home in California, with a wife wearing a white sundress and a

219

daughter with eyes the boys will fall for and curly hair the
girls will envy.
Of course, a job that you'll never have to wear a suit to.
To make sure to marry your best friend – your soul mate.
To make love, not just say it.

If I still love you it must be because we shared at some
flicker of a moment - the same imaginings and the same
soul.

I wish your happiness still included me, but I guess that's
why we called it dreams –
I don't know where we went wrong, or what I have lost,
but I know it was important and it once made us happy.

I hope you think of all of this when you blow out your
candles, which is selfish of me to ask, but I used all my
own wishes up.

Happy Birthday.
I didn't know whether or not to wish you a happy
birthday, just like I didn't know why my heart doesn't
know how to stop caring for you.

Today was your birthday and I didn't dare to call although
I thought about you all day long.

Always,
The Piece You Left Behind.

Oblivious

I'm a believer.
In peace, in joy, in love.
Real – ravenous unconditional beautiful love.
I dance in the moonlight; my eyes are stars.
You are a pretender.
You've tasted lies that you consider the truth.
So you turn away,
what's too painful to know you simply choose to forget.
And you keep your eyes fixed upon him -
pretending, hoping it'll be enough

hope isn't a plan.

The Disappearing Girl.

She immersed herself in him,
she left herself behind
to bring him forward,

and now she sits in a room waiting for him to come home,
waiting for him to say *I love you,*
waiting for him to *embrace her so she would feel
something other than his numb soul touching her body,
leaving her bare, exposed,
shivering as she lays in their sheets wishing she could feel
love radiating from him to her,*
waiting to write words that *mean something,*
waiting for *his* approval.

she left her town, her family,
and thought he was home,
till they unpacked their things
and realized

she lost herself,
she is nothing without him,
she attached herself to him

she looked in the mirror and couldn't even see anyone
looking back.

she was gone.

she collapsed to the floor,
her mind a constant prison,
her '*life*' a filtered perception to fool the world.

Who is she without him?

Addicted

Love is the most dangerous drug.
In a euphoria of pure bliss.
The best narcotic on earth,
all at once soothing and exciting,
pleasurable and painful.

Hooked on a feeling,
High on believing what your eyes mistakenly said.
Till love's effects wear off withdrawing from you,
the alienation and disenchantment that follows,
leaves me empty.

Despite its short shelf life,
love a drug so strong that resistance,
even for the broken hearted, is futile.
The scars, and bruises that are left behind,

I still crave that *high*.

The Story Begins Like This:

Ex-lovers who still care about each other but don't talk
anymore.
They both *think* that each other has moved on -
well... because they don't talk anymore.
Yet they don't know how much one another still cares and
thinks about each other.
**So they walk by each other, pretending their eyes don't
recognize, blocking memories—they wear masks -**
writing and deleting unsent words,
"there's nowhere I'd rather be than with you..."

**too prideful to say, too afraid to admit, to be the first to
put their heart back on the line,**

**I MISS YOU.
I NEED YOU.
I WANT YOU.**

*"I am terribly in love with you, and I always will be, you
stopped saying goodnight and I stopped sleeping"*

*but they are ex-lovers who don't talk anymore, and they
both think each other has moved on..*
So, they end up *drowning* in past memories,
Cursing each other's names to anyone who asks what
happened,
Letting a true love go to *waste.*
Immersing their hearts into new souls yet still feeling
lonely –

longing   for   more.

What a Shame.

An unfinished love keeps you longing for many years,

**well at least they still have
their pride to keep them company.**

Curiosity Killed the Cat

I wonder what he saw in me.
when he looked into my eyes,
every imperfection he fiercely embraced,
I wonder what it was that made him fall in love me.

now I wondered what it was that made him leave me

Astraea

You gave me beautiful sunsets and sunrises but when it
was dark, it was pitch black.

The pavement was cold,
and I stood in the moonlight
you leaned effortlessly towards me
and you took my stars, plucked them from my eyes,
saying that I was too much.
Too much light.

Too bright.
Too happy.
Too loving.

And if I was going to be with you I needed to be dim,
being a star too many people looked my way and it made
you angry -

That I made wishes come true, and brought the lost back
home.
you said if I had that effect on everyone then you couldn't
be special,
even though I let him take my stars to show him I loved
him,

I was *still too bright.*

He knew I was one in a million.

He never found a star that died
and came back to life before.

Years later, we still share them same night sky but he
doesn't know how to look up and not see my eyes.

I can't help but smile,
to know that you think of me every time her pen hits the
page
would you be happy if she skinned me and wore me?
when will enough be enough?
isn't it exhausting trying to be someone you're not?
I guess I wouldn't know what to do either,
trying to convince someone in front of you that the fraud
she considers love is one of the greatest novels of all
time.

Time Machine

I long for a place where courting is alive,
where you weren't expected to take your clothes off to
have fun,
where an emotional connection came before the physical
attachment,
where true love was between two people and not the
world,
I long for a place of just you and I,
a sacred place that no one knows about,
and I think I keep those the most hidden in the pages of
my mind,
written solely for us,
I long for a different time.
there are no ghosts here,
people don't get close to you just to disappear.
I watch movies filled with romance, respect -
there aren't many guys like that,
and why would there be?
In college, I could never fit in, I can't seem to find what
others have found,
pleasure with just sleeping from one bed to another,
but why would men need to be romantic, and date me
and know my inner most thoughts before a night
together?
When I see girls just give it away for nothing?

I can understand why you'd sleep with someone if you
love them, but if you don't know them?
What's the point?

Before he connects with my body, I want him to connect
with my mind, to be attached to me emotionally before
he misses me physically.

I want a man who wants all of me not just parts of me.
it's a new generation,
a new era, of numbness
and I couldn't feel less like I belong,
my soul yearns for another place, another time,
where love was real, and feeling was alive.

The One?

I look in your eyes
and I feel so alive,
but when you walk away,
all I feel are your lies.

"*I love you*". You whispered as you closed the door.

We were ready to try this furthermore.
I leaned in to kiss you once again,
but now how I feel the lies trickle on my lips.

Like the lie you spun when we first begun,
to make me believe you were the one.

Silver Lining

Beautiful things can come out of pain, horrible experiences, out of never ending sadness – but with you, you opened a new part of me, a chapter I never knew existed with words waiting to fill the sky.

Do You Want to Get Tea?

I think of life going by and time passing and I cry.
I cry because everything is so beautiful, I want to soak in every detail like a sponge –
"Do you want to get tea?" she smiles.
Tea is not just a drink for me.
"Tea talks," *tea time*, is a ritual in my family.
Tea holds a Pandora's box of sentiments, creations, security, vulnerability.
When tea time becomes a ritual,
we have the ability to connect with each other,
heart to heart – understanding one another's souls worries, fears, angers and happiness's.
We create art, we make plans,
We appreciate the simplicity, the beauty of ordinary occasions most take for granted, all over a cup of tea.
Tea, it washes our spirits, it's not something that enters our stomach but our minds.
I sit and silently look at my mother,
she's so beautiful – a sunflower radiating, never allowing her petals to weep, her eyes honey brown and hair curly rays of yellow –
she's perfect.
she's everything I want to be.
And we sit here for hours,
hours at a time – days in days out.
Being together.

As far as my mom is concerned, tea fixes everything.

Have a cold?

Have some tea.

Broken heart?

There's a tea for that too.

Sad tummy? Tea for that.

And there it is my dad walking through the door smiling from ear to ear, meeting us for tea after work,

I couldn't think of a man better than this one.

His stature so tall – his heart so wise, so kind – He is a better person than half of the world.

My sister strolls in to pull up a chair, her presence makes my life so much brighter – the protector, the tough armor to my heart, she's the light of my life.

They are my soul mates, my best friends, my heart outside of my body.

And we sit together and I talk with the ones I love the most in the world, the ones I'd always told all my secrets to, the ones I'd want to hide with far away from the rest of the world.

We sit and discuss life, exposed and open.

We know how to set infinity in a single moment.

Who would then deny that when I am sipping tea with my family, that I am not drinking in the universe, that stardust isn't illuminating on our skin,

that with this cup of tea, our little universe is all that matters – I'm safe here, and the rest of the world is quiet.

Who's to say that tea (time) can't do that?

That we can be in our own oblivion sharing anything and everything, sipping tea.

That in this now of me lifting my cup to my lips I breathe in this very picture,

I look at my family, and I'm freezing time,

taking in every detail that surrounds us,
I'm scared.
Maybe that's why I cry, because I can't imagine a life without my parents.
I'd rather die first before having to experience what that will feel like.
I worry when my mom says she tired and my father will never get to be younger the he is now,
I want to cup the world in my hand,
because they are what life is about.
I'm only good at being young.
Time is passing and I want to make it stop,
and I think of the moments that are now memories
and I desperately want to catch them in my hands like fireflies in the summer heat. My mother and father are living proof of the American Dream – of true love, in a world where we laugh at dreams, laugh at the idea of soul mates they defy all the odds.
They have given me the most beautiful map, with treasures and words that have settled in my bones and every day my actions are driven to make them proud – my goals, my dreams inspired by them.
I want to give them the world, grab the stars sprinkle moon dust around them so they have all they need.
I sit here and drink tea and drink in every moment that is happening – I take notes of what they say, they are the wisest of all, my personal little Buddhas.

And one day when I have my family,
I will look at my daughter with a smile and say:

> *"Do you want to get tea?"*

It's okay to feel lost
It's okay to question the universe
It's okay to feel sad
It's okay to feel like your drowning

It's okay to not be okay
But I promise, you will be okay.

Everything will be okay.

Please keep going...

we were such dreamers,

young, and naive we didn't believe that the world had a
dark side, we always heard about it, but never saw what
everyone else cried about.
We fell in love where apples grew, we roamed where
sunflowers never died and blue eyes quenched the deserts
of our hearts.

Than **we** became **I**,
a solo soul traveling life,

I began crying with the world.

hearing the darkness, searching for you in crowds -
but I transformed pain of a past into light to give to others,
illuminating the saddest of eyes.

From suffocating, to breathing.
I was finally alive.

I noticed all the problems that I created are in my head,
the world isn't as dark as the picture I paint.

Dear Anxiety,

I will be honest I'm not afraid of death,
I have a belief, I have a spiritual connection
I know there is more than this.

I'm afraid of time.

The way the clock ticks,
taunting me every second -
I'm afraid I won't have enough of it.

I notice how quickly the hours in the day pass, and the weeks and the months, and years,
the sun sets, the sun rises.

I can't imagine a life without my parents,
they are a soul in me,
when they leave,
I'm not sure if I'll ever be as bright as I was.

I don't fear not falling in love *(again)*
because I noticed I don't need anyone to live,
I don't fear a broken heart because I have had one -
dead and weightless—I revived it myself.

I do fear isolation.
I fear the way I now look at people,

that I put a cage around my heart,
When eyes meet mine I look down,
that I create my own loneliness out of fear that I can't find
what I thought I lost.

I fear people won't understand my soul.
I'm a cluster of starbursts and ancient moons –
that I'm too different, not ordinary enough—
and no one would want the sunflower in a bed of peonies.

I'm terrified that I keep these thoughts bottled up inside
me, that I'm a life sentenced prisoner in my mind, of
worries, 'what ifs'—that this anxiety in my chest is going
to eat at my heart taking away from the beauty of life in
its truest form.

I fear that I have no purpose.
(yet everyone tells me differently)
I fear that no matter how hard I work I will be a failure to
myself.
I fear that I won't feed my hunger,
the depths of my mind that I want to feed -

I want the meaning to know how to end suffering,
answers to the riddles of love and life
I don't just want a career—I want a life.
To reflect at 80 years old and be proud of what I have left.

I fear the word *"happiness"*—
I fear people have taken away the true meaning.
happiness, happiness, happiness.

with the amount of likes on a photo, the portrayal of what people think looks like happiness, a toned body, a vacation in Bali, a mansion.

The preaching of how to be happy, to medicate, to mediate, to appreciate….
I fear people won't shut up and listen to what they are hiding.
Happiness is an internal journey,
love, sex, and people can add to that journey
but I see people have all of it- the *"complete package"*
money, fame, fortune, love,
and happiness is still missing

I fear that I will not be able to unlock the depths of me,
I fear that no one is listening that I'm screaming in a crowded room,

i fear that no one truly cares,
i fear that i care too much, that i feel too much
i fear that my heart on my sleeve is suffering,
being bruised and picked at like a scab for the enjoyment of others —

I fear how the world is changing, and I don't know where I fit.

Yours until I heal,

A constant *(art)* work in progress.

Caged Bird

She's blinded, not by the hate for him but for the hate of
her -
*How can two people move forward if she's always looking
at his past insecure of her future?*

Nothing is promised not even this love she desperately
clings on too, the tighter you hold onto someone the more
likely they want to be **set free.**

A Beautiful Sacrifice

When I'm with you I'm reminded of souls who are pure.
That the sun rises every morning,
that pain is temporary, with you,

you rebuilt me.

My heart didn't feel mangled; you slowly gathered the
pieces from the floor and placed them in my hands.
An overwhelming scent that feels like home struck me.

*"He could never stand next to you, you are too bright, too
beautiful, he wanted to extinguish any fire you had – let
me rebuild what he put out, and I will always let you
outshine me."*

That's what true love is, a beautiful sacrifice.

Love Letter: Love Didn't Hurt You.

Dear "Love Hurt Me",

I think people look at love all wrong, especially when they get hurt. They blame love – love didn't hurt you. Someone who doesn't know how to love hurt you and your confusing yourself between the two.

Love is the most beautiful feeling we can experience – but when relationships end, people lie, cheat, or leave - whatever happens – we get hurt and we blame love. Bitterness sets in and we look at the world differently, those rose-colored glasses you were wearing have been broken and you see the colors you were missing. We truly romanticize the people we adore.

We say, *"I can't fall in love again because I don't want to get hurt."*

What a disservice you are doing to yourself.
Love has never failed you and it won't fail you.

There should be no reason to swear to stay away from it – there are so many people that love us in the wrong ways, who will remind us of the pain that we endured, who create hatred in our hearts – do not let someone poison your soul, do not give the heartbreaker the satisfaction of dimming your shine.

Some people come into your life solely to serve a lesson instead of showing you love.
Thank them because those people are just as valuable as the ones who love you.

People like this only will help you grow taller.
They are the ones who end up lonely – you may think they have the perfect love without you, or that they found what they needed by hurting you – but believe that if you keep your heart on your sleeve and kindness in your eyes, you will end up the richest in life.

There will be a moment they will apologize, and you will get a punch in your stomach and you'll want to drown in the rain rather than deal with the pain of the past – you will feel like pieces of confetti scattered all over the floor, and how they ripped up parts of you that you felt wouldn't never be the same.

We need to accept the feelings we have, the hurt, the sadness, anger – we need to look at them.
Not wallow, not lie on the floor, helpless, but to look at the situation and instead of connecting the person to love being painful, use them to know that is not the kind of heart you ever wanted to love you.

There is so much to be gained without destroying the beauty of what love is really about.

Love never hurts you but the absence of it will.
You may think that without them you are nothing –
do not allow someone to decide what you mean in this world. You are everything.

They will see your beauty everywhere they go, being reminded of what they tried to destroy but never could.

When someone tells you that you mean nothing in this world, they will never be anything more than poor in life. *Riches come from kindness, real love, and truth-you will be the wealthiest of them all.*

Yours truly,

A stronger mind, body and soul.

Self-Worth

I can accept the fact I will always be the girl he loved fiercely, passionately and left behind and never the girl he settled for.

But I won't accept being the girl who broke from someone who didn't know how to love her.

Resurrected

This feeling is alive, back from the dead.
New beginnings are often disguised as painful endings.
I struggled with losing you, an ache for distant places a
craving of your lips.
I have so much left to say to you,
no longer do I want to say it.

      His eyes met mine – and I didn't see you.
A feeling I thought you took,
a skip of a heartbeat,
knots in my stomach hit me – *I breathless.*

You left me with years of loneliness, isolation,
but a boy with brown kind eyes, beautiful soul, euphoric
smile reminded me of what butterflies feel like.
You moved my heart to tears;
I thought I was forever wandering; and it feels so good to
be lost in the right direction.

I thought I knew what a soulmate was,
I thought I had it all figured out,
and my eyes looked upon yours and something happened
not cosmic, not out of breath
but serenity - I felt calm

for the last few years I have been wanting to be alone,
I would look down at every eye that met mine,
any person who would get close I turned my back away,
I was avoiding the world.
But with you,
I don't want to be that person

I want to look you in your eyes,
and hear your laugh
talk about your hopes, dreams and
protect you from leprechauns.

there is something about your soul that draws me close to
you,

I want to know your deepest
secrets and be the reason
the crease smiles from your eyes,

what I'm trying to say is that I like you,
you make me feel at home,

am I talking too much?

Two atmospheres don't collide on accident.
I wish on every star that our universe now will allow us to
be those two kids who once drew lines in the sand,

How desperately I hope this life lets me cross it.

Naked Body Naked Thoughts #NoFIlters.

Intimacy and love aren't harder to find,
it's just harder to find people who are willing to be naked with you.
Naked with emotions, with thoughts, fears, and dreams.
To find someone to truly trust, to be exposed and vulnerable.

#Nofilters.

We *swipe left and right, looking for the best image to capture our eyes.*
But try to find someone to fall in love with you emotionally before a physical attachment — that's a challenge.

But what can I expect when we live in a world where we filter a sunset?

You'll share a bed with a body but won't tell them you like ice cubes in your cereal for extra cold milk, because that makes you weird.

You'll give parts of yourself but won't talk about how your favorite time of the day is right before the sun sets and the moon rises. That you think the moon stares at the sun in awe of her beauty right before she goes to sleep — a forbidden romance. Because that makes no sense, and why would anyone care?

You'll lie naked next to a person but refuse to send them a text first; you have to follow the 'rules', because you don't want to look 'clingy' or 'desperate'.

We expose our bodies but hide our thoughts, our personalities, filtering our hearts.

But it's okay, because everyone "*doesn't care*", and it's "*all having fun*" a new generation of no feeling, no commitment.

It's about pleasure, to have your cake and eat it too.

How about you stimulate my brain?

But what can I expect when we live in a world where we filter a sunset?

I'll still take my sunsets flaws and all, heart bleeding red #NoFilters … extra ice cubes in my cereal, staring at the moon in awe of the sun — sending the **first** text.

Sometimes I wish I could sleep for a long time, tranquilly sedated from pain, from intrusive thoughts, healing my wounds.

And when I'm ready I'll awake like a caterpillar in a cocoon, emerging as a beautiful butterfly.

Superwoman

I know probably from time to time he looks up my name,
hoping I'm sad, or that my glowing eyes have dimmed –
but the only thing he will see is a girl he doesn't recognize.
A girl who can finally be herself. I took parts of myself to
make him grow, lowering my shine, to make him the sun.

He saw glimmers of my corniness and dorky ways – but
constantly censoring herself to make him feel grand.

A girl who used to say she *'likes'* writing but he never
knew it was her passion. That words to her were like
orchestrating music – sweet sounds you could not only
feel but hear if written with precision.

A girl who told him she wanted whatever he did.
She thought that was what love was, to give him the world
while she watched from space.

But now he will see words that will punch him right in the
core and leave him breathless:
he will see her happy eyes and contagious smile;
he will see that the girl he left behind is and will always
be the sun and he will never eclipse her ever again –
now he is watching her from space.

Solo

My heart beats for me only; the blood pumping through my veins is to give me life.
These beats you hear are my personal song and melody- we do not share that rhythm.

Selfish?

It was selfish to believe that people's hearts beat for each other –
we all have different sounding rhythms –
it's when we hear a tune that flows with ours is when beautiful love is made,
an instrument to accompany an already striking solo act.

Unchained Heart

For a long time, I was bound,
suffocating in chains from you.
The lamb fell in love with the lion.
Our story binds us.
We both moved on,
but even when we try to forget one another
                    our love will remember.
When we left each other where did our love go?
We tuck it away.
And I feel you forget me,
and I watch your life in pictures,
we have gone separate paths
you put my love at the bottom
storing it away like a love letter in the wall.
I have scars left from you,
they have slowly healed,
I've set myself free,
unchained from your love.

His Regret.

if they ask you about me, tell them:

"She was the only person who loved me with honesty, and I broke her."

Wildfire

Young love is a flame;
very beautiful, very passionate and intense, but only flickering,
blown to an end with the slightest breeze.
True love,
real love from a disciplined heart is a deep burning, ravenous wildfire.
It can withstand the winds of hurricanes:
it is not as easily dimmed,
not as easily blown to be left just smoke lingering in the air.

Love Letter: Anatomy of Love.

Dear Heart,

What happened? What did I do to you?
You were so prestigious, a science.
A noble prize winner.
Regarded as the most important organ,
Electricity going through my heart makes the muscle cells contract.
But all I remember was the kiss that sent my heart into arrhythmias.

Four chambers to you:

The upper chambers called the left and right atria,
the lower chambers the left and right ventricles.
A wall of muscle separates the left and right atria but what do I feel now?
That love and hatred can exist side by side in this septum.
That the left ventricle – the largest and strongest chamber in my heart is now demolished,
there are strings in the human heart that should not have been tugged – no matter how tough the armor appears.
The left ventricle's chamber walls have enough force to push blood through the aortic valve and into your body.
Now I barely feel a pulse, the energy that once was there transferred to another.

When I was young, I knew where my beats were, placing my hand on my chest – I was alive.

According to science it was simple.

But this wasn't science, this was love, and love in the human heart feels things that science can't see, knows what the mind can't understand.

But how do I repay you?

I turn human anatomy into sunflowers, stars and salty kisses.

I dissect the heartbroken mind, transferring it to the body in metaphor, prose, and poems.

I selfishly ignore the beauty you give me every second of the day, never resting, never falling short – and in the present you aren't broken – but always beating, continuously no matter how many times I have metaphorically broken you.

Faster from excitement, slowly to enter a field of dreams. Harder to help me through my days, never once faltering, he didn't break you.

I did.

I'm sorry,

but I felt things his heart couldn't, I turned to science to heal but that is logic,

and love isn't logical.

Thank you, for still growing sunflowers despite him planting weeds all over our chambers.

Deepest Apologies,
The soul that resides in you.

Misunderstood

Never expect your heart to be understood by all, people might relate but understanding comes through living and we all live differently.

You look at me through a screen, through words people have whispered into your ears, through jealously, your own insecurity - so you dislike me all on your own.

I wish you a kind heart,
I wish your eyes to know that we are all humans with feelings, fears and desires.
I wish you knew that we are more alike than different.

Closure

I have loved you since we were kids –
do you remember that feeling?
I still have that for you.

I love you - I always will
but,

it wasn't meant for us - here, this time, this universe
another life we are together; I feel it in my soul.

    it's not your fault people leave -

Love Is Change.

How do you get passed the big fight?
with tears, the hurtful words exchanged,
when the yelling simmer's down to silent breaths over the phone
where your laying and blankly staring at the ceiling and you hear:

"You know I love you, right?
Tell me we will be okay, tell me it'll be fine
nothing will change, we will still be us."

But that was the problem we needed to change each other.

It's the moment you believe that love is not about losing or winning, or egos.

You're a team, you are best friends.

Love is truly just a few moments in time, followed by an eternity of situations to grow from,

love on the contrary to what people believe is change.
It's the moment in the relationship that had become not just a destination but a lifelong quest to keep watering each other, and growing for one another.

Relationships aren't movies,

falling in love is not enough,
staying in love will always be work,
realizing you can't survive just on love.

He said he doesn't change....

Who he was at 17 is who he is at 23, and who he'll be at 30. I couldn't understand that logic, to me life is about change. To adapt, to evolve, to learn, to love someone other than yourself.

But to fall in love we have to take risk of changing yourself for this person—you are giving them power to change you—your soul knows that—there is an egotism between two, yes, we deserve that honeymoon period where it's rainbows, cute and perfection all the time, but love has to expand, has to grow, has to change you.

If you don't change each other— how could you ever love.

Every love you have is an opportunity,
the gift is in the interaction and the connection with this person, whether it lasts forever or not.

I was a caterpillar when I met him in a cocoon of his world—and now that I became a butterfly he's upset because his high school dreams never went too far.

Creatures of Habit.

There are two phrases that humans seem to exhaust in this era:

I love you, and I'm sorry –

That's why I'll spend my life searching for new ways to express overused words that seem to have lost feeling and meaning in this generation.

She was the sunflower he loved in the summer
the letter she wrote him in May,
she sent him her heart in August hoping a grand gesture
would keep him from going away.
But she already felt the brittleness in her leaves,
and he let her drown in her tears and be restrained in her
mind,
while the fall leaves kissed the ground he threw a knife in
her stem
dropping over in the garden,
he plucked one petal, *"do i love you?"*
another he plucked *"i love you, not."*
till she stood wilting over,
he took her last petal and put it in his pocket,
he whispered under his breath,

"I love you....

not."

Love Blinds You.

As the old tale goes, love is blind.

When you're falling in love, everything your love does and says is interesting and amazing. You're wearing a smile from ear to ear plastered from a witty text and good morning kiss, and every word from their mouth is pure poetry, every move they make, is magical.

First love blinds you to red flags, and even when you do notice them, you're quick to sweep them under the rug. We are quick to forgive because we believe that our love can do no wrong because love is forgiveness, right?

Well, memory reminds me to open my eyes.

I never felt worthy of something without the feeling of
him, he left the flowers of his broken
heart hidden in the wall.

Love sick since he abandoned the heart he named the
intense sky of his earth,
logically he needed to stop the inexplicable complacent
woman who killed the wonders of his smile,
how she believes their simplicity from a past history of
attachment will act to resemble a mindful love.
He is married now, but his horrific crying from her
suffocating peonies chokes his lungs.

One day he breathed out sunflowers and saw yellow
peering out of his veins,
flashes a reminder of regrets that were conceived when
he plucked her last petal and whispered
"I love you not," as she wilted over,

he ran to the ocean screaming to the waves
pulling the dead weeds from his lungs,
finally,
breathing in his simplicity of his paradise he missed so,
the sand, the waves kissing his feet,
the sun who he had not seen in years -
begging for her return,
shouting of the desires he shoved in the back of his soul,
out of his pocket her last petal,

     I love you,
          he declared to the sun.

Agapé Love

Just because you were mean, doesn't mean I will speak ill of you.

Just because you ignored me, doesn't mean I won't smile as you walk by on the street.

Just because you didn't understand my heart, or me doesn't make me creepy or weird.

Just because you can't fathom that the world is made of people who care of others, doesn't mean I'll stop caring.

Just because you broke my heart, doesn't mean I won't love again.

Just because you don't understand how much I've hurt doesn't mean I won't heal.

Just because you have Ms. Right Now, doesn't mean Ms. Right will be waiting.

Just because we can't be together, doesn't mean I won't love you.

> *Just because I love you,*
> *doesn't mean I want you.*

you don't just throw people away,
yet you recycled me over and over again
and then you dumped me in the ocean
but I came back as the waves kissing the shore.

Pave Paradise

*"She'll never get old. Just as the sun never gets old.
She's the one that makes my day begin"*

In that moment, staring at his words, I cried.

I cried because he was the one I always dreamt about, the words I wrote in the air hoping would manifest into something real, someone real.
I cried because you make me feel like the sun again when I didn't think I would ever feel like anything but a small star in the sky.
I cried because I hope I can be what you need because you are what I need.
I cried because when I was pushing away,
you pulled me in closer
loving every broken part.

I cried because I believed that *this* feeling was forever gone.

In that moment,
I felt my heart re-bloom,
once sunflowers were planted in my lungs, choking me.
Now, a new soul has touched my heart and watered the parts of me that was left to die,
taking my fallen petals,
taking my weeping face,
bringing me back to life

looking me straight in the eyes *"my heart is yours,"*

In that moment, I cried.
I have found someone who accepted all of me,
not just parts of me,
who didn't leave trails of hope,
who gave me hope.

Who gave me love
when I didn't want to give any.

I have found a man who has found beauty in even the
darkest parts of me.
Sharing his dreams, his heart,
I found a person who has taken me by my hand,
who entrusted me with their soul,
who wants to walk together
side by side,
in our secret garden
paving our way to our own paradise.

Celebrate The Love
That Hurt You

"Sometimes the beauty is in the attempt, you tried everything, you fought and it still didn't work..."

Celebrate the love that hurt you.

celebrate the person who couldn't love you right.
The one who kept you guessing and lead you on,
who would kiss you and under the same breath say,
"we are just friends",
Who would say *"I love you"* and disappear,
Who made you feel like a desperate version of yourself.

Celebrate that you recognize and see now what inconsistent, unbalanced love does to a person and remember to never give it yourself.

Celebrate in knowing you are better off without that kind of love,
celebrate to know that love changes and shifts, just like life.
So sometimes *"the one"* isn't really *"the one"* and just a lesson needed in that moment of your journey.

Celebrate that love had power to move you and that's how you know it was real—**it changed you.**

Celebrate that you know how to hold a heart without breaking it.

Instead of crying tears of hurt
pop a bottle, put on your beautiful smile
and celebrate what you gained, not lost—
you lose nothing, they do.

Celebrate that this insane, crazy, miraculous life is much
more than just one unbalanced love -

celebrate that you deserve more.

It's not about writing about someone who left,
it's not about rewriting what happened,
it's writing the truth of the story that was selfishly taken
when my heart was shattered,
silenced by you.

LOVE LETTER: FINALE

The May Letter.

"A bad love letter asks for love back; a good love letter asks for nothing..."

Dear John,

I know you are probably thinking why the hell is she writing me?

But I know if I texted it would go unanswered, or maybe you blocked my number, as we have blocked one another from our lives, pretending we do not exist to each other.

You can't block memories, you can't block history— you can block the present to avoid the truth of the past, so I'm sending you this letter…

The truth is that I have suffered without you.

I have grieved immensely.

if I were to take your face in my hands, look in to your light blue eyes and say to you with the most gut-wrenching sincerity that these scars will never fully go away,
you would still have no idea what it was like to despise waking up in the morning because you were not in my life anymore.

A bad love letter asks for love back; a good love letter asks for nothing back.

With you out of my life, I have become the person I neglected when I was immersed in you.

You engulfed me for a long time, you have no idea the pain you imposed.
The agony that was in my chest cavity, that was in my mind.

I lived my days hoping, waiting –

The sad thing was even after everything I still believed that you were different.
That you wouldn't treat me this way, that you valued me as a human, as a person, as your best friend to look me in the eyes, to tell me that you never wanted to see me again.

I suffered from the repercussions of a boy who selfishly attached himself to only leave me with my heart bleeding out of my chest.

I laid awake endless nights replaying the last phone call in my head.
I have to constantly relay on my memory of words spoken, of texts sent,
going back rereading our old messages to find if there was a part of you that actually loved me.

I wish I was enough for you.

But at first, all I was seeing was the desperation of a girl who wanted a boy to love her so much that she was vomiting words to prove her love for him.

To show that he was the one she wanted and he was just dragging her along, exaggerating the truth, hiding the fact he knew that she was never going to be in his life, keeping her around for the selfishness of his own pleasure, his own ego.

Why did you decide to violently take my soul and
suffocate any ounce of sunlight I had left?
Is this what you planned?
Viciously hurting me to a point of disgust?
Is this the ending you wrote out for our story?

You spit on my name, belittling my worth, my character
and I couldn't believe what a coward you were,
you were a disappointment that night.

I was worth a goodbye,
I expected that you would take my heart and hold it in a
cocoon in the coarse callus of your hands even at the
ending of our journey.

I was worth more than the insanity you began to spun.

Making up words, making up lies to show that the heart
that writes before you now, was some insane
brokenhearted girl, that she was as you said
"crazy, creepy and weird"–

When in reality I realized,
 it was never me,
       it was *you.*

That you could paint me in whatever light you wanted
when deep down you knew the truth,

you had fallen in love with me.
You were the one who was broken, damaged,
for having to end the best thing you would never have.
Covering your pain with any absurdity that would make
me look like a fool, and you a King.

Trying to convince yourself that if you stabbed me with
the cruel sound of your voice

that destroying our history would make the present of
your past easier to navigate.

You were, just as shattered as I was when we parted
ways –
The only difference was you had another to distract your
mind and body,
what an empty feeling.
You can pretend you never knew me,
you never have to breathe my name again,
but just know that I accepted you unconditionally for
who you were,
and never once picked away pieces of you,
as you did with me.

I will never apologize for who I am.
For being there for you entirely,
for my frizzy curly hair.
For being the awkward, smart, witty,
dreamer, innocent girl, full of life, full of optimism –
I will never again apologize for being everything that
you as an insecure boy couldn't handle.

In the end, you weren't enough for me.

I am proud of the woman I was then, and have grown
into now because of your half-filled love.
A woman you will never know.

You may be able to go from person to person without a
second thought.
For a while I was confused on why someone who
carelessly and cruelly wants to hurt others gets to feel
loved – and then I realized that that the love you have is
not real. I feel sorry for you.

I loved you so much I took the sun out of the sky for
you, I would capture the moon if you asked,

I want you to be happy more than I want the sun to rise
in the morning,

I took pieces of me and gave you them to help you grow,
I was killing myself and
you kept giving me the rope instead of cutting me down.
Why didn't you want to save me?

Was it her that made the world brighter instead of me?
Was my presence never enough?
Why did you choose to let us slip away?
What did you see in me that you couldn't see in your
future?

You have the ocean in your eyes,
you crave an adventure but your shipwrecked.
You don't need anyone,
as I learned, I do not need you.

You use validation from relationships to feel important,
to feel something that is missing from your soul.
I wish one day you find what is it that will fill you up
more than just the superficial act of temporary
satisfaction that you lay with at night.

I know you have searched for me in another person,
and you still haven't found her, and you won't.

It's very simple.
You may think I hate you now, or spite you,
or all the things that happen when a person you once
love becomes the stranger they started with: but you are
wrong,

Without you moving onto the next chapter without me I
wouldn't have been fulfilling my own destiny,
I wouldn't be where I am today.
Us writing our own chapters without each other is the
most beautiful story we could tell.

We are both human. we both made mistakes,
I know you can't express with words like I can,
and I know that I at one point suffocated you with my
verses, and I'm sorry for that but,

you were truly a part of me - at times I do miss you in
the most desperate human way, and I close my eyes and
I long for the past, and I wish I took in the moments of
us more.

I guess I always believed in my gut that we would have a
lifetime of infinite days together.

I wish I could remember what it was like to feel your
kiss, or more so I wish I could feel us in that way with
no words, no touching – just how our energies would
combine through the windows of our souls, how we
were connected,
our own secret love song.

That we found a love that was more than physical,
a love that was so passionate, a love that was accepting
of differences, and the only time we fought was when we
knew we wouldn't be together.

All I have engraved in my heart is the hate you spewed
on me in 9 minutes.

No matter how long time goes by,
with each new day that I awake too

I will have memories of you that come to me out of the
blue, and they will suffocate me some days,
and they will comfort me others,
but I know if this happens to me,
your remembering me at times as well.

I will forever be in love with the person I first met
I don't recognize this man now
you have a new individual who has changed the mind of
the one I fell for.
I hope he returns, not for me – but for himself.

You loved me in the way you knew how, and I don't
hold that against you,
I used to ask why,
I used to hope for an answer from you,
for an apology
and now I want nothing from you.

I thank you for opening me up to what this word *"love"*
can do to a person,
the dimension and depths it holds and I experienced that
because of you.

I experienced that you will not be my only love,
that I will find an amazing human who's going to know
how to hold me and unlike you,
won't let go.

You will never know this soul that writes these words
before you,
you will never have had the chance to fully be loved by
me,
and for that I feel sorry for you.

I wish you the most beautiful life, the most
encompassing love,

the happiness you told me you wanted,
I hope you get everything you told me you dreamed of,
I was always rooting for you, and I always will.

But mostly I wish, and
I hope one day our eyes will meet in passing and instead
of looking down we will smile at each other,
knowing that even if I couldn't be the love in your life,
that even though years passed, and we never had our
proper good bye –
I can smile knowing I was the love of your life.

I had so many dreams wrapped up in you,
you will forever and always be the love that changed me.
The pain I endured, the broken soul I healed on my own,
the story left unfinished, the poem I keep writing...

you are my love letter I keep hidden in the wall.

I have exhausted every word, every metaphor, every
ounce of light left in me for you to show
that you were my once everything, my best friend and
I want to thank you from the bottom of my core,
I know we were soulmates in this life.
I was to challenge and awaken you, and you did the
same to my soul, we evolved into a higher state of
consciousness being together.

Yes, you broke me, but I came back as the sun, and
every time you try to forget me
I rise again each and every morning,
but no longer do I rise for you.

Even if our love couldn't see through for years to come –

you will always be my Agapé love.

I love (d) you.

Acknowledgments

To my beautiful mom, dad, and sister – thank you for always believing in me when I couldn't. For your unconditional love and support. For always telling me I can accomplish anything. You don't even realize what your presence means to me –you are my world. God has blessed me with the most unbelievable soul mates. Without you this book would never have been possible. To my yiayia Demitra you asked me the simplest most striking question, *"Does he have a good heart?" "As long as his heart is beautiful, so is he"*. I keep that tucked in my mind during life's journey, and keep you in my heart every day, s'agapo poli. I miss you every day.

To my second sister Ceci Gallogly, I will never meet another person like you - you are incredible. You are there for me when the rest of the world doesn't get me. I can't begin to tell you what sunshine you bring to me. Thank you for accepting me and for our entire sisterhood. Thank you to my big Greek family and all my friends who I love so deeply. Thank you to everyone I have met in my life. Thank you to the kind hearts, and even the misunderstood hearts who've had an effect on my soul.

Demetra Demi Gregorakis is a writer and a lover of poetry. She writes about an Agapé love, which she owes to her beautiful parents, married 30 years, who have shown her the definition of unconditional love. Writing has always been her calling; hoping her words will bring back feeling to millennials who have gone numb from technology.

There are these little memories throughout her time she wishes she could keep in jars: flashes of moments, people, specific places that she wishes she could relive, which bring her heart to her stomach – that make her 20s the most confusing, lonely, amazing, time of her life. She captures her experiences and lessons in *Love Letters in the Wall*.

One can say she's dreamer or a hopeless romantic – or just an old-fashioned girl trying to fit in this world where commitment has become feared, love is a convenience and conversations are texting. Whatever it is, her heart is a thousand years old and she's not like other people. She opens her soul for the world to read – sharing her own personal heartbreak. She hopes her words empower, and inspire that heartbreak, love and the journey we go on is only one aspect of your story – you are whole all on your own.

Continue to follow more of Demetra's adventures at
demetrademi.com
tweet a love letter @demetra_demi